Witch Is When The Bubble Burst

Chapter 1

"You're doing it again," I said, trying to sound as miffed as I felt.

"What?" Kathy gave me her 'who me?' look. "What am I supposed to have done now?"

"You're sticking your nose into my love life."

"I didn't think you had one."

"I don't, but—"

"Then I can hardly stick my nose into it, can I?"

I hated it when Kathy insisted on dragging logic into an argument.

My name is Jill Gooder, and I'm a P.I. I'd taken over the family business after my adoptive father died. My life had become much more complicated when I'd discovered that I was a witch. I wasn't allowed to tell any human about the whole witch thing, and that included my adoptive sister, Kathy.

"Look—" she said.

It was never a good sign when Kathy began a sentence with the word 'Look'.

"You and Jack Maxwell were getting on just fine until Susie what's-her-face showed up. But now she's gone, so you have a clear run at him."

"It's not as straightforward as that."

"Of course it is. You either like Jack Maxwell or you don't."

"Even if I did, and I'm not saying I do. But even if I did, he hasn't actually asked me out."

"*You* could ask *him*."

"No way."

"I could ask him for you then."

"Don't you dare. I still haven't forgiven you for rigging the raffle."

My phone rang.

"It's him." My throat had suddenly gone dry.

"Maxwell?"

I nodded — still staring at the phone.

"Answer it then!"

"I'll let it go to voicemail."

Kathy snatched the phone out of my hand, and before I could stop her, she'd pressed the 'answer' button.

"Jill Gooder's phone," she said in a sing-song voice. "Hello, Detective Maxwell! It's Kathy, Jill's sister."

I shook my head, and mouthed the words, "Tell him I'm not here."

"Yes, she's here. She'd just nipped to the loo, but she's back now. I'll pass you over."

Kathy handed me the phone; she had a huge grin on her face.

I gave her a death stare, and whispered, "I'm going to kill you."

"Jack. How are you?"

"I'm fine," he said. "I just wondered if you'd like to get a coffee some time?"

Kathy could hear both halves of the conversation, and was nodding like one of those stupid dogs that people used to have in the back window of their car. What? You still have one? Sorry — obviously nothing stupid about those at all. Lovely little things.

"Jill?" Maxwell said.

"Sorry. Kathy was distracting me. Sure, why not?"

Kathy fist pumped the air. So childish.

"How about tomorrow afternoon?"

"See that wasn't so painful, was it?" Kathy said, once I'd ended the call.

"I guess not."

"He must be keen if he got rid of Sushi for you."

"Who says he did? She was probably transferred back."

"Come on, Jill. How naive are you? He obviously did it for you."

Susan Shay or 'Sushi' as I preferred to call her was an ex-colleague of Jack's. She'd been assigned to the Washbridge force for a while, and had made things very difficult for me. I wasn't sure if Jack had been instrumental in having her sent back or not—it was a nice thought, but I wasn't entirely convinced.

Jack Maxwell and I may have buried the hatchet, but we were hardly starry-eyed lovers—we hadn't even kissed yet. And besides, there was still Drake to consider. If what his brother had told me was true, I'd treated Drake badly. At the very least I owed him an apology.

"Earth to Jill." Kathy nudged me. "Dreaming of Jack?"

"We're just getting coffee. That's all."

"For now." She smirked.

Kathy got a call from her husband, Peter. While she was distracted, I sneaked up to Lizzie's bedroom. It was a stupid thing to do. When Kathy had guilt-tripped me into handing over my collection of beanies to my niece, I'd made her promise to keep them out of sight, so I wouldn't be tortured by seeing their demise each time I visited. And yet, there I was sneaking in to her bedroom so I could get a look at them.

Oh no! I wished I hadn't.

There were beanies everywhere: on the bookcase, on the bedside cabinet, on top of the wardrobe, but mostly on the floor. But that wasn't the worst part. Kathy and Lizzie had developed a Frankenstein complex, and had begun to create 'hybrid' beanies by joining two beanies together to create what I can only describe as mutants — monsters. What was this one meant to be? I picked up the hideous looking thing.

"That's a Zebodile." Kathy had sneaked in behind me.

"It's horrible."

"I kind of like it. It was Lizzie's idea to match the zebra with the crocodile."

"Have you thought of taking her to see a therapist?"

"She doesn't need a therapist. It shows she has an active imagination. That's a good thing."

"This?" I held the monster at arm's length. "You think this is a good thing?"

"Sure. Why not? At least she has fun with them. That's more than you ever did. You were too busy cataloguing them to actually enjoy them."

There was no arguing with her. What did she care that I'd be having nightmares about Zebodile and his monster friends for months to come?

"There you go." Kathy held out a Tupperware box, which contained only custard creams.

"What's going on?" Alarm bells were already beginning to ring.

"What do you mean? I thought you preferred them this way. Untainted by other biscuits."

I did—it was true. What worried me was why Kathy had chosen now to do it. She'd never pandered to me before.

"What do you want?" I said, after taking a couple of biscuits.

"You're so suspicious, Jill."

"I know you. What do you want?"

"Well, you remember you promised to have the kids while me and Pete go away for the weekend?"

"Did I?"

"Come on. You know you did. For our anniversary."

"Oh yeah, your anniversary—I remember now. But that's ages yet."

"It's this weekend."

"It isn't. It can't be. I'd have remembered. I went to the wedding."

"That's funny—so did I. And it's definitely this Saturday."

When I'd agreed to have the kids, the anniversary had seemed an age away. I'd figured there would have been enough time for me to come up with an excuse, but then I'd forgotten all about it.

"Don't look so worried," Kathy said. "As it turns out, I'll only need you to have the kids on the Sunday. You can manage that, can't you?"

"How come?"

"They're going to the seaside on Saturday with one of our neighbours. They have a boy and a girl, about the same age as our two."

"What about Saturday night?"

"Don't look so worried. They won't be staying at your precious show home."

"I wasn't worried." Terrified more like. Goodness only knew what havoc my nephew and niece could cause.

"Anyway, they'll be back late, so Courtney's mum said they can stay at her place."

"Courtney's mum?"

Kathy laughed. "I don't actually know her first name. She's always been Courtney's mum. Just like I'm Lizzie's mum or Mikey's mum. Anyway, the kids are going to have a sleepover there. You just need to pick them up on Sunday morning, and keep them entertained until we get back in the evening. Do you think you can manage that?"

"Of course."

"Why the long face, then?"

I shrugged. "I'm a just little disappointed. I'd been looking forward to having them for the whole weekend," I lied.

"I could always talk to Courtney's mum, and —"

"No! It's okay. Sunday will be fine."

Dodged a bullet there. How bad could it be for one day?

***

When I got back to my flat, I was so busy thinking about my upcoming coffee date with Maxwell that I let my guard down. I didn't spot Mr Ivers approaching from my right until it was too late to make a getaway.

Mr Ivers was one of my neighbours. He was obsessed with movies, and could bore for England.

"Jill!" He was grinning, which was rather unusual for him.

"Mr Ivers. Nice to see you. Can't stop. I left the bgghrh on the sggegt," I mumbled.

"Sorry?"

"I don't want it to burn." Back to mumble mode. "The bgghrh."

I should have known better than to think my feeble attempt at an excuse would put him off. He was clearly a man on a mission.

"I have news," he announced.

"That's nice."

"Aren't you going to ask me what it is?"

Might as well get it over with. "What's your news?"

"I've been offered my very own newspaper column."

"That's great." In Insomniacs Monthly no doubt.

"I'm so excited. The Bugle are very keen."

I should have known. The Bugle was the local rag which was to journalism what sardines were to — err — journalism. They both employed fishy tactics and they both stank.

"I gave them a copy of my newsletter," Mr Ivers continued. "They liked it so much they've asked me to do a regular column."

"Are they going to pay you?"

"No, but I get to see all the movies I want for free which means I can cancel the monthly subscription for my movie pass."

"Good for you. I'm really pleased for you."

"I do have some bad news though." His face was suddenly solemn. "I may have to discontinue the newsletter. I realise that would come as a disappointment to all my subscribers."

Both of them.

"I may not have time to write the column, and publish the newsletter. Hopefully it won't come to that."

"Hopefully."

I'd signed up for his ridiculous newsletter in a moment of weakness when I'd felt sorry for him. I hadn't actually read any of them. I'd tried to put one in Winky's litter tray, but he'd threatened to tear my hand off if I brought it anywhere near him.

"You could always take out a subscription to the Bugle." His smile had returned.

"I'll definitely give that some serious thought." Believe that and you'll believe anything. "Well, it's been lovely talking to you. I have to get off."

"There is one more thing, Jill."

With Mr Ivers, there was always one more thing. My will to live was slowly ebbing away.

"The Bugle wants a photograph for the column."

"Of you?" Wasn't their readership plummeting enough already without actively scaring readers away?

"Yes. I think maybe I should have a make-over first. Hair cut, new suit—that kind of thing. You always look fashionable—"

At last. Someone had noticed, even if it was only Mr Ivers. I was slowly warming to the man.

"Perhaps you could come and take a look at my wardrobe?"

"I suppose so." What do you mean two-faced? Why shouldn't I give the poor man the benefit of my advice? It was the least I could do.

"What about your bgghrh on the sggegt?" He appeared concerned.

"What about the what on the what?"

"You said you had bgghrh on the sggegt."

"Oh, yeah. I just remembered. I took it off before I came

out."

"Great."

"Lead the way."

"I don't think you've been in my flat before, have you?" Mr Ivers said.

"I don't think so."

Oh deary me. Did you ever watch those TV programmes about hoarding? Yes, then you get the picture.

"Come through to the bedroom!" he called from somewhere behind several piles of newspapers.

Now there's something I never expected to hear from Mr Ivers.

"Where are you?" I shouted.

"Straight ahead until you reach the Big Screen Monthlies, and then take a left."

I followed the directions, and was relieved to find his bedroom was clutter free. It was, however, not purple free. Everything was purple. The walls, the carpet, the bed covers — everything.

"I can guess your favourite colour," I said, trying not to sound as freaked out as I felt.

"It's yellow."

I laughed. Who knew Mr Ivers had a sense of humour?

"It's true," he said straight-faced. "I love yellow."

I'd long had this theory that different people saw different colours when they looked at the same thing. Kathy had always mocked my theory, but maybe this was the proof. Maybe Mr Ivers saw purple as yellow.

"Yellow?" I glanced around. "You mean like this room?"

He looked at me as though I just rode in on the crazy stagecoach. "This room is purple."

"Yeah—I know—I meant—never mind. Shall we see what's in your wardrobe?"

The man was beyond any help I might be able to offer. His clothes spanned the decades, and somehow he'd managed to pick the worst from each.

"I thought a pin-stripe suit with the red and yellow cravat," he said, holding said cravat under his chin.

"No one wears cravats any more."

"I thought maybe I could spark a revival."

"This is going to take a lot more work than I thought," I admitted.

"I don't have long."

"I know, but you want to get it right don't you?"

"Of course. I have my readers to consider. I don't want to disappoint the ladies."

"Quite. Why don't you leave it with me? I'll give it some thought and get back to you."

He looked disappointed, but said, "Okay then."

I took a couple of wrong turnings on my way out, but eventually made it back to the land of the sane. Advising Mr Ivers was way beyond my capabilities, but I thought I knew someone (make that *someones*) who could do it.

Chapter 2

"You're looking exceptionally pleased with yourself, Mrs V," I said.

I hadn't seen her look so happy since the regional knitting competition, which she'd won despite my inadvertent attempt to sabotage her scarf.

Mrs V, my PA/receptionist (allegedly), spent most of her day knitting. She specialised in scarves, and was something of a celebrity in local knitting circles.

"I am feeling quite chipper. I've had a letter from an old flame."

It was probably ageist of me, but somehow I found it hard to envisage Mrs V with a man. There had been the unfortunate incident with the sailors when she and Grandma had a night out on the tiles, but she couldn't remember anything about that.

"His name is Donald."

"That's a nice old fashioned name."

"Donald Hook."

I laughed. "Sorry. He must have had a tough time at school."

"What do you mean?" Mrs V's smile had been replaced by a puzzled look. "I think Donald is a nice name."

"It is. I wasn't laughing at that. It's just—you know—Donald Hook—quack, quack." I laughed.

Mrs V didn't.

"I still don't know what you mean," she said.

"Come on. With a name like that he must take a lot of stick."

"No, not really."

Just me then.

"So, what did Donald have to say?"

"He wants to visit. He's asked me to go for lunch with him."

"Very nice. Were you and he once an item?"

"Not exactly, but we came very close."

"What happened?"

Mrs V began to tidy her desk. "I don't remember exactly."

I didn't buy that, but I didn't feel like I should press her.

"Do I have anything in the diary this afternoon?"

She checked. "Mrs Rhymes at three thirty. That's all."

"Good. I'm going to be out early afternoon. I have a meeting with Detective Maxwell."

"Really?" Her face lit up again. "It's high time you two got together."

"We aren't getting together. It's just a business meeting."

"Of course, dear. Will you be wearing those?" She looked disapprovingly at my green top and skirt. It had taken almost half an hour for me to choose this outfit.

"What's wrong with these?"

"Nothing. Maybe you should ask your sister for fashion advice? She managed to snag herself a man."

My mouth opened and closed like a goldfish, but no sounds came out. There were so many things wrong with that statement; I hardly knew where to begin. Ask Kathy for fashion advice? I was the only one in the family who understood fashion, or had any taste. Snag myself a man? I could snag myself a man if I wanted to—granted he'd probably be a narcissistic, cheating, loser. But even so—I knew how to attract the opposite sex. Didn't I have two men competing for my affections right now?

I didn't care what Mrs V thought, I liked my green ensemble, but I needed a second opinion. From someone a little more knowledgeable in matters of fashion than Mrs V.

"Winky? What do you think of my outfit? Do you think I look hot?"

Winky, my one-eyed, psycho cat, glanced across from where he was sitting on the leather sofa.

"Meow, meow."

"Don't just meow at me. I need your honest opinion."

Ever since I'd inherited my witch powers from my birth mother, I'd been able to talk to Winky. For a feline, he had good fashion sense — particularly when it came to eye patches which I noticed he'd discarded today.

"Meow, meow."

He jumped off the sofa, walked over to me, and began to rub against my legs while purring at high volume.

Something was amiss. Winky was acting strange — for him. Acting like a normal cat in fact. Winky never did that.

"Stop messing around. I need your opinion."

"Meow, meow."

I glanced over at the window sill. That was where Winky normally kept his little flags. He'd taken to using semaphore to communicate with Bella, his catwalk model girlfriend, who lived across the way. There was no sign of the flags.

"Meow, meow." He continued to rub against my legs.

What was going on? Had he reverted to being a 'normal' cat? Could I possibly be so lucky? Might I actually be able to focus on my work instead of having to worry about what he was going to get up to next?

This day was getting better and better.

By early afternoon, Winky was still acting—err—normally, I guess. By that I mean he was still acting like a cat.

"I'm off to meet Jack Maxwell," I said, as I left the office.

Mrs V gave my outfit another disapproving look. "I should make sure you go somewhere with subdued lighting."

Charming. "By the way. Have you noticed anything different about Winky?"

Mrs V shrugged. "What kind of thing?"

"He isn't—I mean he doesn't—I don't know. By the way, did you move the flags?"

"What flags?"

"Never mind. See you later."

***

Jack Maxwell was waiting for me outside the coffee shop.

"Green suits you," he smiled.

"What do you mean by that? What's wrong with green?"

"Whoa!" He held up his hands. "Who bit your bum?"

"Sorry. I thought you were—sorry—I've been having kind of a strange morning."

"I thought 'strange' was your default. Anyway, I meant what I said. Green does suit you."

"Thanks."

Jack insisted on buying the drinks—I pretended to

object. The coffee shop was quiet except for the usual posers with their shiny, metallic laptops.

"I was sorry to hear that Sushi's gone," I said, trying my best not to smile.

"I doubt that. It's a shame that you two didn't hit it off. Sue is exceptionally good at what she does—"

"Get up people's noses?"

"See, you do have something in common."

"Touché. So, if she's so good, why did you get rid of her?"

"We both felt it would be for the best."

I wanted him to admit it was because he wanted to spend time with me, but he was never going to do that.

"Does that mean we can go back to our previous relationship?" I said.

He grinned. "I wasn't aware we were in a relationship."

I blushed. "I meant our *professional* relationship."

He grinned some more. He was obviously enjoying my self-inflicted discomfort.

"You know my feelings about private investigators," he said.

"They aren't top of your Christmas list?"

"My feelings haven't changed, but—" He took a sip of coffee. "I'd be a fool not to recognise that you've contributed to a number of recent high profile arrests."

You think? Solved them all single-handedly more like.

"For that reason, I'm prepared to allow you a little leeway, but the old rules still apply. You do not get in the way of my investigations, and you bring everything you have to me. Understood?"

"Aye, aye, sir." I gave him a little salute.

"And cut the smartassery."

"Now you're asking the impossible." I smiled. "Everything else I can live with."

"So we have a deal?" He offered his hand.

"Deal."

I liked the feel of his hand on mine. Now if only I could get those lips on mine too.

"Refill?" he asked, but before I could say yes, his phone rang.

"Maxwell."

He listened, and the longer the call went on, the more serious his expression became.

"Where? When? Okay, I'll be there in ten."

He finished the call, stood up, and almost as an afterthought turned to me.

"Sorry. I have to go."

"Something serious?"

But he'd already gone, along with the promise of my second latte.

***

"Why does that cat have to be out here with me?" Mrs V sighed. "You know how much he hates me."

"Mrs Rhymes is allergic to cats. You know what happened last time."

Mrs Rhymes was a sweet old dear who thought her husband of close to fifty years was cheating on her. When she first came to see me, I almost had to call an ambulance because she couldn't stop sneezing. She sneezed so much that she could hardly draw breath. I'd had no idea she was allergic to cats, and she hadn't spotted Winky who was fast asleep under my desk. It was only when he popped his head out to see what all the noise was about that she was able to let me know what the problem was. I didn't want a repeat performance, so this time I planned to get Winky out of my office before the old dear arrived.

Winky was still acting strangely. And by strange, I mean like a normal cat. He wasn't talking to me, he wasn't using semaphore to communicate with his girlfriend, Bella, and he hadn't ordered anything online for several days. He was meowing and rubbing against my legs. I'd begun to wonder if maybe my magical powers had disappeared, but I tried a few spells and they seemed to work okay.

"He's been on his best behaviour," I reassured Mrs V, as I lay him down under the radiator in her office. It was the furthest point from the linen basket, which was full of yarn.

"I don't trust him." She eyed him suspiciously.

"Look." I pointed to Winky who had curled up, and looked ready to sleep. "He won't be any trouble."

"He'd better not be."

Before Mrs Rhymes arrived, I sprayed my office with a 'neutraliser' spray which I'd bought specially. It promised to get rid of any airborne allergens—it had better work—it had cost me an arm and a leg.

"Mrs Rhymes, how nice to see you again."

Short, big-bosomed, and with hair that had a mind of its own, Mrs Rhymes reminded me a little of Aunt Lucy.

"I've been dreading this," she said, as she took a seat. There were tears in her eyes, and I was pretty sure it wasn't due to her allergy. "I'm not sure I want to know the truth."

"I think you'll want to hear this." I smiled.

"You mean. Ronald isn't — ?"

"Your husband isn't cheating on you."

"Are you sure? He's been acting so strangely recently. Going out in the evenings. Ronald never goes out in the evenings."

"I believe it's your wedding anniversary soon?"

"Yes, fifty years; our golden wedding. That's what makes it all the worse."

"I followed Ronald. He's been taking dancing lessons."

"Dancing? Ronald can't dance. He hates dancing."

"The course of lessons he's been taking is usually for people who want to be able to lead the first dance on their wedding day. It's specifically targeted at beginners. Do you have a celebration planned for your wedding anniversary?"

"Yes. We've booked the Regent Hotel. Family and friends have all been invited."

"Will there be music?"

"Yes, a four piece band."

"There's your answer then. I think Ronald plans to surprise you on the day."

"Oh my goodness." She reached for a handkerchief.

"You have absolutely nothing to worry about. Your husband obviously loves you very much."

"Oh my goodness. I feel terrible for thinking badly of him. Does he know I had you follow him?"

"No. I was very discreet. He need never know anything about this."

"Oh my goodness. I'm so relieved. How can I ever thank you?"

"No thanks necessary."

"What about your bill? I wouldn't want you to send it to the house."

"I assumed not." I opened the drawer, took out the bill which Mrs V had prepared earlier, and slid it across the desk to her. "There you are."

Mrs Rhymes floated out of the office.

"Another satisfied customer," Mrs V commented, after she'd left.

"Pity they can't all be like that." I glanced over at Winky who didn't appear to have moved. "How was he?"

"He's never moved. Never made a sound."

"Been good as gold then?"

"I still wouldn't trust him as far as I could throw him."

Chapter 3

I was spending more and more time in Candlefield, which was home to all manner of supernaturals (or sups for short). It was feeling less like somewhere I visited, and more like a second home. Having two different families was great. In Washbridge I had Kathy, Peter and the kids while in Candlefield I had Aunt Lucy and the twins. Oh, and Grandma of course. How could I forget Grandma? It's a serious question—how could I forget Grandma? All suggestions on a postcard, please.

"Have you forgotten that I can read your mind?" Grandma said.

"Morning, Grandma. How are you on this beautiful day?"

"My bunions are giving me gyp."

Gross! "Isn't there a spell which could help?"

"Why gosh. I never thought of that."

Whoops. Me and my big mouth.

"Thank you Jill for that brilliant suggestion."

"I just meant—"

"You realise you have another test coming up soon?"

How could I forget? "Yes, Grandma."

"I expect you to be thoroughly prepared."

"Yes, Grandma."

"Good. Well, I can't hang around here all day. I need to find Lucy, so she can treat my bunions."

"Bye then." Lovely to see you too, Grandma.

"I heard that."

No sooner had Grandma disappeared than the twins came charging down the street towards me.

"You were hiding," I said.

They both giggled.

"We saw you with Grandma, and thought we'd wait until she'd gone," Amber said.

I did a double-take. Amber had a beauty spot on her cheek which was the only way to tell the twins apart—except today they both had a beauty spot.

"Amber?"

"Yes," they both said, then dissolved into giggles.

"Come on you two. What's going on? Which one of you is Amber?"

"I am," they both replied. And giggled again.

"Sorry Jill." Pearl wiped off her 'beauty spot'. "We couldn't resist it."

"Very funny. You should have tried it on Grandma. I'm sure she would have found it hilarious."

"We're not that crazy. She looked in a bad mood."

"Isn't she always? Her bunions are giving her gyp."

"I hope I never get bunions." Amber screwed up her face.

"You've already got them," Pearl said.

"I do not. That's where my new sandals rubbed."

"Sure looked like a bunion to me."

"It's not. Anyway, at least I don't have crow's feet."

"I do not have crow's feet." Pearl's hand automatically went to her face. "I don't, do I?" She looked at me.

"Not that I can see."

I stood between the two of them before things got out of hand. "Enough you two. You're both beautiful. Except when you squabble. I come to Candlefield to relax—not to act as referee to you two."

"Sorry, Jill. It's her fault."

"Yours more like."

"I hate being a twin."

"I hate being *your* twin."

"Right. That's enough," I said. "I'm going back to Washbridge."

"No, Jill. Please, don't."

"Don't, Jill. Please."

"I'll only stay if you two pack this in."

"Sorry."

"Yeah, we're sorry."

"Okay. I'll forgive you, but I need a favour in return."

"Anything."

"Name it."

"It will mean a visit to Washbridge."

"Yay!"

"We love it there."

"There's a guy in the same block of flats as me. He's—well, he's sort of—he's kind of—. Well anyway, you'll see for yourself. He's got himself a gig writing a newspaper column for the local rag, and he wants a makeover before he has his photo taken for the column. I thought you two might be able to help."

"Sure," Pearl said. "We'd love to."

"Is he hot?" Amber asked.

"Mr Ivers? Not really. Anyway, you shouldn't be asking that." I grabbed her hand, and touched her engagement ring.

"I was only asking." Amber blushed. "You know I wouldn't cheat on William."

"You would if Jethro asked you out," Pearl said.

"I—err—I."

"Amber?" I pushed her.

"Of course I wouldn't. Jethro is hot though."

"Scorching," Pearl agreed.

I'd heard tales about the legendary Jethro who looked after Aunt Lucy's garden, but I had yet to meet him. From all accounts, I had a treat in store.

"What kind of column is your friend going to be writing?" Amber said.

"Funny you should ask. You and he should get along just fine. He's going to review movies for the Bugle. He used to produce his own newsletter."

"Really?" Amber looked genuinely impressed. "That's my dream job. I can't wait to meet him."

It couldn't be often that anyone said that about Mr Ivers.

"I'll speak to him and let you know when he'd like you to come over."

We made our way to Cuppy C, the twins' cake shop and tea room. I kept Amber on my right and Pearl on my left. I figured there was less chance of them fighting if they had to go through me.

"What's going on over there?" I pointed to the scaffolding and boarding on the property directly opposite Cuppy C.

"We're not sure," Pearl said. "That shop has been empty for some time. They started work on it last week."

"I don't believe it!" Amber yelled when we drew closer. "Look!"

"No!" Pearl stared in disbelief at the newly erected sign above the shop.

"Best Cakes?" I said, as the three of us came to a halt directly opposite.

"Why would they open here?"

"It isn't fair."

The twins were staring in disbelief at the white and blue sign.

"I shouldn't worry." I tried to sound cheery. "You're already well established. Your customers won't desert you."

Pearl ran across the road, read the small notice which had been pinned up, and then sprinted back.

"It opens next Wednesday. Lots of opening offers it says."

"This is war." Amber huffed. "We'll show them who has the 'best' cakes."

"We can hold a sale on that day too."

"Dead right we will."

This was fighting talk. If nothing else, the new shop had brought the twins together with a common purpose.

Let the cake wars commence!

The twins were busy plotting their campaign against the new shop, so they declined the offer to accompany me when I took Barry, my Labradoodle, for a walk. Aunt Lucy and the twins had bought Barry for me, and they looked after him here in Candlefield whenever I was in Washbridge. How can I put this nicely? Barry wasn't the brightest button in the box, but he was adorable all the same.

"I want to go for a walk." He jumped around in circles with excitement.

"We're going."

"When?"

"Now. Right now."

I began to put on my trainers.

"I want to go now."

Oh boy. As soon as I'd clipped the lead to his collar, and opened the door, he dragged me towards his favourite place—the park.

"I love the park!"

"I know you do."

"I love to walk."

"Yeah. I know."

"I love to walk in the park."

Adorable, but not the world's most engaging conversationalist, that's Barry.

"Do you remember what I told you last time?" We were in the park, and he was raring to get off the lead.

"I remember."

"And the time before that?"

"I remember."

"What did I tell you?"

"Don't go too far. Don't go out of sight."

"Good. You promise?"

"I promise."

"Okay. There you go—Barry! Barry, come back!"

That dog would be the death of me. Every time we came to the park, he did the same thing. Every time he promised not to run off, and every time he did. I knew he *could* behave because he'd done it at the dog show. The problem was he seemed to pick and choose when to take any notice of me. Well, enough was enough. I'd spent the last twenty minutes chasing after him. This couldn't go on.

Back at Cuppy C, the twins were still discussing their strategy for the cake war campaign.

"Hi, I'm back!" I shouted.

No reply. They were both too engrossed in the paperwork on the table in front of them.

"Yes, thanks. I had a nice walk," I said.

Still nothing.

"A handsome vampire asked me to marry him, but then an even more handsome werewolf said I should run away with him instead."

I was obviously talking to myself, so I fed Barry, and then checked the Candlefield Pages which was equivalent to the Yellow Pages. There had to be something in there.

Sure enough there were several entries under the 'Dog Obedience' section. I picked the one with the picture of the cutest dog, and gave them a call.

'No Bones About It' offered a six part group course, and they had a new one starting the following Friday, so I booked a place for Barry and me.

There wasn't much point in hanging around in Candlefield. The twins were so preoccupied with their cake wars strategy they wouldn't have known if I was there or not.

***

Winky was still being really weird—even Mrs V remarked upon it.

"It's like he's taken a 'normal' pill," she said. "He even rubbed against my legs and purred when I fed him. He never does that."

Even though I was curious as to what was going on with Winky, I had other things on my mind. There was an article in the Bugle which had caught my eye. It related to the kidnapping of Amanda Banks, daughter of Dexter Banks, the hugely successful and very rich industrialist. As soon as I read it, I realised that must have been the subject of the call which Jack Maxwell had taken when we were in the coffee shop. His whole demeanour had changed instantly which was hardly surprising given his history. The reason he had such a downer on private investigators was because one had royally screwed up during another kidnapping with the result that the hostage had been killed. Jack Maxwell had been the lead detective on the Camberley kidnapping case, and the death of the hostage had hit him hard. It was obvious from our discussions that he laid the blame for her death at the door of the P.I. who'd been acting for the family.

It would probably be better for all concerned if I stayed out of his way until this case had reached its conclusion. Hopefully this one would have a more positive outcome.

***

"Mr Ivers!" I shouted. This was a first—I was chasing after him instead of trying to avoid him. "Mr Ivers. I'm glad I caught you. I've had a word with my two cousins, Amber and Pearl—"

"Amber and Pearl?"

"Yes. They're both very fashion conscious, and more abreast of the latest trends than I am."

"Yes, I had noticed you're a bit stuck in the sixties."

Cheek of the man. "Anyway, they've agreed to come over to give you the full makeover."

"That's very kind. Thank you."

"No problem. Oh, and by the way. Amber is a big

movie fan. I'm sure she'd love you to talk her through some of your recent reviews."

How could I be so cruel? Snigger.

"Really? Does she like any particular genre of film?"

"I believe she's partial to paranormal. Werewolves in particular."

I was still chuckling to myself when I got back to the flat. Amber would probably kill me, but I had no doubt Pearl would find it funny.

That's when I remembered.

Tomorrow was the day I had to look after Kathy's kids. All day! How had I allowed myself to get talked into this? I knew it was their anniversary, but even so. Surely they would have enjoyed it more as a family. What did kids like to do anyway? As far as I could make out it seemed to be: scream, shout and generally be a pain in the backside. I had to come up with something to keep them occupied, and it had to be something that kept them as far away from my flat as possible. Under no circumstances did I want those two little — err — darlings — back here.

Chapter 4

After much research, I'd decided to take the kids to Daletown Manor Park which was an hour's drive from Washbridge. I'd never been there before, but it appeared to be a stately home which had turned its grounds into an amusement park. There was a farm with lots of smelly animals, and a children's play area. Hopefully there would be enough there to keep the little *darlings* amused for the day. First though, I had to collect them.

"You must be Jill." I was greeted at the door by a woman about the same age as Kathy.

"Hi, yes. And you must be—"

"Courtney's mum." She laughed. "Caroline actually, although hardly anyone calls me by my name."

"Auntie Jill!" Lizzie came running out of the door, and gave me a big hug.

"Look what I've got!" Mikey shouted, and held aloft a toy drum.

"I hope you don't mind the drum," Caroline said. "Some parents aren't very happy with Trevor's choice of toys. Trevor's my husband. He can be an idiot some times."

"I'm sure Kathy and Peter will love it." I laughed. "Well, thank you for having the kids overnight. I had hoped to have them for the whole weekend."

"Yeah, your sister said something like that." She grinned.

Busted. I should have realised that Kathy would have briefed her on what a terrible auntie I was.

"Where are we going, Auntie Jill?" Lizzie shouted from

the back seat. "Can we go to the seaside?"

"I want to go to the movies," Mikey yelled.

"The seaside is better than the stupid movies."

"Seaside stinks. I want to go to the movies."

"Movies stink more than seaside."

This was going to be a long day. Maybe I could use the 'sleep' spell? No! What was I thinking? I'm such a terrible person. But then a little doze couldn't do any harm, could it? No! Kathy would kill me.

"You went to the seaside yesterday. We're going to Daletown Manor Park today."

"What's that?"

"It sounds boring."

"Are there any movies there?"

"You'll both like it. There's a big house we can look around."

"Boring!" Mikey groaned.

"I want to build sandcastles," Lizzie said.

"There's a farm with animals and lots of rides." I did my best to sound enthusiastic.

"Mummy said we'd have fun. That's not fun."

"It will be. You'll see."

I cast the 'sleep' spell.

Mmm, lovely peace and quiet. What? So sue me, I'm a terrible person.

I reversed the spell when I saw the sign for Daletown Manor Park.

"Are we nearly there yet?" Mikey yawned.

"We're here. You two lazybones have been asleep."

***

"*How* much?" I must have misheard.

The young man with a runny nose and a lisp sighed. "Twenty pounds for adults. Ten pounds for under tens."

"I want to look around, not buy the place."

"Do you want a ticket or not?"

"Can the kids go in while I wait out here?" What? Kathy wouldn't have minded.

"Under fourteens must be accompanied."

"They'd be accompanying each other."

He shook his head.

"Hurry up, Auntie Jill." Lizzie pushed me from behind. "I need a wee-wee."

I handed over the cash, took the tickets, and once inside, led the way to the toilets.

Daletown Manor Park had seemed much more impressive in the photographs. It had looked much bigger, more colourful, and the animals hadn't smelled nearly as bad.

"Why are you holding your nose, Auntie Jill?" Lizzie said as we walked along the path through the farm.

"It smells."

"That's the pig poo."

"And the cow poo," Mikey added.

"And goat poo."

"And Llama—"

"Yeah, thanks. I get it. Lots of poo. Maybe we should go and look around the house?"

"That's boring." Mikey groaned. "Houses are boring. I want to go on that!" He pointed to a hot air balloon which was on a square of grass to our left. The sign read: '*Hot Air Balloon Rides – every two hours – adults: £10, children: £5'*.

"It's too dangerous." I'd never been fond of heights.

"Are you scared?" Mikey said.

"Of course not. I just don't think your mummy would want you to go up in a balloon. Come on; let's take a look around the house."

"Boring."

Lizzie pretended to snore.

"But, I've already paid," I protested.

"That ticket covers entrance to the grounds, not to the house."

"How much is it?"

"Ten pounds for adults—"

"Let me guess. Five pounds for children?"

"Seven fifty actually."

"Daylight robbery."

"Do you want a ticket or not?"

"I want to go on the hot air balloon instead," Mikey shouted.

"One adult's, and two children's tickets for the house, please."

The kids had been right; the house was boring. Buckingham Palace it was not. Uninspiring paintings hung on dusty walls. Unremarkable furniture filled room after boring room.

"I'm bored," Mikey said for the tenth time. Lizzie was too comatose to complain. This wasn't going to play out well when Kathy asked the kids about their day. Maybe there was still time to redeem things at the fun fair. Perhaps I could use magic to win them cuddly toys like I had at the colonel's garden party. Yeah—that's what I would do.

The kids were so relieved to get out of the house that they ran ahead.

"Hey! Wait for me!"

They ignored me of course. I lost sight of them when they rounded the wall.

"Where's Mikey?" I said, still trying to catch my breath.

Lizzie giggled.

"Lizzie! Where's your brother gone?"

She giggled again, and then pointed to the grassed area.

"Where, Lizzie?"

"In the balloon."

I spun around to see someone untying the last of the ropes which tethered the hot air balloon to the ground.

"Stop! Wait!" I yelled as I ran towards the balloon. I couldn't see Mikey, but then the basket was rather deep. He was probably hiding so I wouldn't see him and drag him out of there.

The last of the ropes was released, and the balloon began to rise.

"Stop! Stop!" I threw myself at the basket just as it left the ground. The pilot stared at me in disbelief as I hung on for dear life. I glanced down—that was a mistake.

"Here!" The pilot grabbed one of my arms. One of the other passengers grabbed my other arm. Between them they managed to haul me unceremoniously into the basket.

"What do you think you are playing at?" the pilot yelled at me.

I was looking all around, trying to spot Mikey. "Mikey?"

"Who's Mikey?" the pilot asked.

"My nephew. He sneaked into the balloon. Mikey?"

There were maybe a dozen people in the basket, but I couldn't see Mikey.

"How old is your nephew?"

"He's seven."

"There are no children on this trip."

"Are you sure?"

"I'm positive."

I pulled myself to my feet and looked down to the ground where Lizzie and Mikey were waving to me. Even from that distance I could see them laughing.

I hated kids. Cruel and sadistic—all of them. As the balloon continued to gain height, I could see them making their way towards the funfair. I couldn't let them go in there by themselves.

"How long does this trip last?" I asked.

"It's an hour long."

"An hour? I can't be up here for an hour!"

"You should have thought of that before you jumped on board. Oh, and by the way, you owe me ten pounds."

I handed over the money, but my pleas to turn around fell on deaf ears. I had to get back on the ground somehow. If the kids told Kathy I'd let them go into the funfair alone, she'd skin me.

It was time for magic!

When I'd seen the 'heavy' spell in the book of spells, I'd chuckled to myself. What a useless spell, I'd thought. When would I ever want to make myself heavier? Lighter, maybe, but never heavier. Looks like I was wrong.

It was just like being in the hall of mirrors where some of them make you look fat. The difference was this time I actually was getting fatter. My arms, legs and whole body blew up like a — pardon the pun — balloon. Pretty soon the other passengers had to move to the edge of the basket to make way for my enormous body.

"What's going on? What's happening to you?" the pilot said.

"I have a rare allergy to heights. It makes my body swell."

He looked confused — hardly surprising.

"We'll have to go down," he shouted. "There's too much weight."

"Sorry," I said to the other passengers who were all staring at me like I was some kind of freak show exhibit.

Five minutes later, we touched down. As soon as we did, I reversed the spell, and climbed out of the basket.

The pilot stared at me in disbelief.

"The allergy soon subsides once I'm on the ground," I said, before sprinting towards the funfair.

I caught up with the kids at the big wheel.

"Can we go on there, Auntie Jill?" Mikey said, as though nothing had happened.

"I want a word with you two."

I grabbed them by the hand, and marched them over to a quiet corner.

"What was that all about?" I demanded.

They both giggled.

"It's not funny."

"I could see your knickers when you were hanging from the balloon," Lizzie said, and they both giggled again.

"You told me Mikey was in the balloon."

"It was just a mistake."

More giggling. Those two were getting as bad as the twins.

"What would your mother say if I told her what you did?"

"I don't think Mummy would be happy that you went in the balloon, and left us all by ourselves. We were scared, weren't we Lizzie?"

"Yeah." Lizzie pretended to shudder. "Scared."

"I don't think we need to tell your mummy about this." Kathy would eat me alive.

"I'd like a toffee apple," Mikey said.

"I'd like candy floss and a toffee apple."

"Then we'd like to go on the big wheel."

This was blackmail. Well, if they thought they could blackmail me, they had another—

"Or we'll tell Mum about the balloon."

"Toffee apples and candy floss it is then."

Needless to say, the fun fair stalls and rides were not included in the ticket price. By the time we made our way back to the car, I was out of pocket by another fifty pounds.

***

"Mummy!" Lizzie screamed as she ran towards Kathy.

"Mummy. We went on the big wheel."

"Did you? That sounds exciting. Where did you go?"

"To some boring house with animals, but the fun fair was good. Auntie Jill paid for us to go on everything."

The kids disappeared into the house.

"Did she now? That's very kind of her." Kathy turned to me. "You look shocking."

"Thanks. I'm beat. I don't know how you do it every day."

"You get used to it after a while. Where did you take them?"

"Daletown Manor Park."

"I've seen the ads for that."

"Don't believe the hype."

"The kids seem to have enjoyed it. I hope you didn't spend too much."

I managed a weak smile. I daren't even think about how much the day had cost. "Did you and Peter have a good weekend?"

"Really good, thanks. We both said we should do it more often."

She must have seen the expression on my face because she laughed. "Don't worry. We'll get someone else to take them next time."

"They were no trouble," I lied. "I barely knew I had them."

Peter walked down the drive to join us.

"I hear you had a good weekend," I said.

"We did, but not as good as you apparently. Lizzie tells me you took a trip in a hot air balloon."

Busted!

Chapter 5

On Monday morning, Mrs V was still as chipper as ever.

"Have you heard any more from The Captain?" I smiled at my own joke — someone had to.

"Captain?"

"You know. Hook. Captain? Get it?"

"Oh, right. Very droll. Donald is taking me out for lunch tomorrow. You'll be able to meet him then."

"I'd better watch out for the handshake." I laughed.

Mrs V didn't; she just shook her head.

"How's Winky?"

"He's been as good as gold."

Coming from Mrs V that was praise indeed. I should have been pleased, but I was starting to worry. What had happened to the psycho, crazy cat I'd come to love and hate in equal measure?

"Hi, you!" I called to Winky as I walked through to my office. He was lying on the sofa.

"Meow." He jumped down and began to rub against my legs.

I crouched down. "What's going on, boy?" I tickled him under his chin. "Why aren't you talking any more? Are you okay?"

"Meow, meow."

"Did something happen to you? What's wrong? Why aren't you talking?"

"Meow, meow."

"Maybe I should take you to the vet. But then, what would I say: 'My cat isn't talking to me any more'?"

"Meow, meow."

"I'll get you some milk."

I stood up, and began to make my way over to the fridge.

"It had better be full cream."

"It is—" I spun back around. "You can speak again!"

"I was just messing with your head. You're so gullible." He was rolling around on his back and laughing.

"This was all a joke?"

"I have to do something to amuse myself. Seeing as you won't take me home with you, and I'm stuck in this office all day long. I even had the old bag lady fooled. She called me her little darling this morning." He rolled around in hysterics.

"You're evil. Do you know?"

"Aw come on. Where's your sense of humour? It was funny, and anyway, it sounded to me like you've been missing our little tête-à-têtes."

"In your dreams."

"Don't pretend you weren't. Didn't you just say that you might take me to the vet?"

I slammed the fridge door shut.

"Hey! Where's my milk?"

"Sorry. All out."

I held out for another thirty minutes before I gave in to his constant complaining. The full cream milk did the trick. I would never have admitted it to him, but I had kind of missed his banter. Yes, he drove me mad some— strike that—most of the time, but I hated the thought of going back to purrs and meows. Lapping up the milk had obviously worn him out because he was now fast asleep on the window sill. Mrs V would be in for a nasty shock when she realised he'd reverted to his loathsome self.

"Jill!" Mrs V's voice crackled through the intercom.

Rather than waste my breath trying to get her to hear me, I walked through to the front office.

"This gentleman would like to see you. He doesn't have an appointment. I told him you were busy."

In his late teens, maybe early twenties, the young man was wearing ripped jeans and a blue shirt. With his deep blue eyes and floppy fringe, he would have looked good in anything.

"Please, Mrs Gooder," he said. "This is really important."

"It's Miss. Come on through."

"Young man," Mrs V called to him. "Take this." She handed him a blue scarf to match his jeans and shirt.

He looked at me; I shrugged.

"My name is Steve. Steve Lister."

"Take a seat, Steve. What can I do for you?"

"I've read several articles about you recently. About how you caught the 'Animal' serial killer and stuff."

There never was a serial killer, but if the myth brought in the punters, who was I to disillusion them?

"It's my girlfriend," he said.

Of course it is. It always is.

"She's been kidnapped."

Alarm bells began to ring. There weren't that many kidnappings in Washbridge, and I had a horrible feeling that I knew who his girlfriend was.

"Amanda Banks?"

"Yes, how did you know?"

"I saw it in the Bugle," I said.

"That's where I read the article where you slammed the Washbridge police for being incompetent."

"I didn't actually—"

"Well you're right. They won't tell me anything, and they don't seem to have a clue. That's why I need your help."

"I'm really sorry, but I can't."

"I have money. Whatever you charge, it isn't a problem."

That would have been music to my ears normally, but this was different. With any other case I wouldn't have hesitated, but a kidnapping? Knowing what happened with the Camberley case, there was no way I could take this on if I wanted to maintain any kind of relationship, professional or otherwise, with Jack Maxwell.

"It isn't the money. Look, I'm really sorry, but I'm snowed under with work at the moment. I just wouldn't be able to give enough time to the case. I'm really very sorry."

His face fell, and it felt like I'd kicked a kitten.

"Sorry," I said again as he left.

"Another satisfied customer," Winky quipped after the young man had gone.

Contrary to what I'd told Steve Lister, I wasn't actually that busy. The anticipated influx of business following my recent high profile cases hadn't materialised—at least not in the numbers I'd hoped for. The kidnapping case would have been a great one to get my teeth into, and I was still annoyed at having to turn it down. Jack Maxwell had better appreciate the sacrifices I was making for him.

While things were quiet, I decided to put in a little magic practise. I'd been playing around with the 'move' spell recently. It was fairly simple in that it allowed me to pick up and move objects using only the power of thought. As was often the case, the problem lay not in performing the spell, but in refining it in such a way that I had tight control over exactly where the object was moved to. It was simple to lift a pen off my desk and place it on the sofa, but if I wanted to move it to a specific spot, that was way more tricky. Curiously, I found it was more difficult to be accurate with smaller, lighter objects than with more solid ones. That's why I decided to try it on Winky's little flags which were now back on the window sill. He was staring out through the window, and the flags were right behind him.

Here goes.

I cast the spell, and then focused on one of the flags. Gently and slowly I raised it from the window sill. Winky was so engrossed with whatever he was looking at that he didn't notice it start to float towards my desk. I wanted to lower it onto the A4 pad which was on the desk in front of me.

"Hey!" Winky yelled.

The noise almost broke my concentration, but I managed to regain my focus just in time.

"What are you doing with my flag?"

"Shush! I'm trying to concentrate."

"And I'm trying to reply to Bella. She's just made a rather interesting proposal, and I need to tell her yes."

"Shush! You'll have to wait."

"This can't wait. She might change her mind." He began to signal with his solo flag. "She doesn't know what I'm saying. Give it back."

"Shush! Nearly done."

The flag was now hovering over my desk. A little fine

adjustment was necessary to make sure it hit the right spot.

"Hurry up!"

"Quiet!"

Slowly it came to rest on the A4 pad—result!

"Give me that flag!"

"There you are."

He snatched it from my hand and began to signal frantically.

"Damn it! That's your fault," he shouted at me. "She's changed her mind now. She said I'd taken too long."

"Sorry." I laughed.

"You will be."

I spent the next hour refining my technique on the 'move' spell. I didn't use Winky's flags again—it would have been more than my life was worth. He was desperately trying to persuade Bella to give him another chance. Part of me wanted to ask what exactly she'd proposed, but another part of me thought I was better off not knowing.

"I have a bone to pick with you!"

I was so startled that I lost focus on the paperweight which was floating across the room, and it crashed to the floor.

"Grandma? Where did you spring from?"

She'd appeared in my office out of thin air. I shouldn't have been surprised—she had a habit of turning up out of the blue.

"Never mind where I sprang from. What about my bone?"

"What bone?"

"The one I have to pick with you."

"I have no idea what you are talking about. What am I supposed to have done?"

Winky's fur stood up and he hissed at her. Grandma pointed a finger at him, and he froze. Like, literally froze—as though he'd been turned to stone.

"You 'froze' Winky!"

"Who?"

"Him. My cat."

"He's okay. He was getting on my nerves."

"Reverse the spell."

"All in good time. First you and I need to have a talk about Trading Standards."

"Trading what?"

"Standards. You know—that thing which young people no longer seem to care about."

"What about Trading Standards?"

Grandma sighed, walked across the room, and took the seat opposite mine. "I had a visit from the charming people at Trading Standards this morning."

"I don't understand."

"Someone had told them that Ever A Wool Moment is involved in some kind of scam."

"What kind of scam?"

"They say that we're using false advertising when it comes to Everlasting Wool."

Grandma had opened a wool shop in Washbridge. Her latest initiative was Everlasting Wool which was a kind of subscription service for yarn. Think Spotify or Netflix— then think wool—and you kind of get the idea. No? Don't worry, no one else understands how it works either.

"So are you going to deny it?" She pointed a crooked

finger at me. At least, I think it was pointed at me—it was hard to tell.

"Yes, I'm going to deny it. Why would I dob you in to the authorities?"

"Dob me in? How old are you? Five?"

"I haven't spoken to Trading Standards."

"You sent them an email then."

"I haven't spoken to them, and I haven't sent them an email."

"An anonymous letter?"

"Grandma, I promise. Whoever reported you to Trading Standards, it wasn't me. Cross my heart and hope to die."

"That could be arranged."

"What?"

"If I find out you're lying—but then there are worse fates than death. I have a long list of them."

"I promise it wasn't me. So what did you tell them?"

"I've managed to fob them off for now, but they say they'll be back to investigate further. Let's see how much further they get when I turn them into cockroaches."

"You can't do that."

"Slugs then. Makes no odds to me."

"If Everlasting Wool is above board, you won't have anything to worry about."

"Are you suggesting it isn't?"

"No, but—"

"But what?"

"But I can't figure out how it works."

"That's why my business is a success, and yours—" She looked around the office. "What is your business anyway? Do you actually have any customers? The only people I ever see in here are Annabel and that thing."

Poor old Winky was still doing an impression of a statue.

"I have plenty of clients, thank you very much. There was one here no more than an hour ago."

"What is it you're working on for him?"

"Well—err—I didn't actually. I couldn't—"

"I rest my case."

With that she stood up and made her way to the door.

"Wait!" I yelled after her.

"What is it? Some of us have a real business to run."

"What about Winky?"

She sighed, pointed a finger at him, and then left.

Winky looked dazed. "What happened? It feels like I'm stoned."

Chapter 6

"Are you okay?" Winky shouted from the window sill.

"Yeah. Why?"

"You keep smiling to yourself and grinning. It's a little unnerving."

"I'm fine. Thank you for caring."

"I didn't say I cared. It's just that it's off-putting. I need to keep my focus in case Bella gives me another chance."

I couldn't stop thinking about Grandma. I knew it wasn't nice, but a small part of me thought she'd got the comeuppance she deserved. Everyone in Candlefield banged on about how important it was not to allow humans to know about sups, and yet there she was flaunting her magic like she just didn't care. Trading Standards—so funny. I couldn't help but wonder who it was who reported her. And why I hadn't thought of it first.

The door opened, and Mrs V walked in. Her happy demeanour hadn't lasted long.

"You have to do something about that noise, Jill. I can't concentrate. I've dropped three stitches already this morning."

I'd been hearing the banging for some time, but with the door to the outer office closed, it had been muffled. It sounded much louder now.

"What is it?" I started towards the door.

"It's those people from next door. They're moving in."

Armitage, Armitage, Armitage and Poole was a firm of solicitors based in the next building. Their business was apparently flourishing and they wanted to expand. Gordon Armitage had tried to persuade me to vacate my office, so they could move in. There was no way I'd ever give up Dad's old office, so I'd refused. He wasn't best pleased. The other residents of my building had been more accommodating, and had accepted a payment in return for moving out. It appeared that Armitage was now in the process of moving in.

I could barely squeeze out of the door. The landing and stairways were blocked with the removal men who were delivering dozens of desks to their new premises.

"I don't think my asking Gordon Armitage to quieten things down will help. Knowing him, he'll probably ask the removal men to make even more noise. Hopefully, it shouldn't go on for too long."

Mrs V harrumphed. "They'd better be done by tomorrow. I don't want my Donald to get caught up in it."

"He's still taking you out for lunch then?"

"Of course. I'm quite excited."

It was nice to see Mrs V so thrilled about her date. At least one of us still had what it takes.

"Jill!" Gordon Armitage called from the doorway. "Sorry about all of this noise. I do hope it's not disturbing you too much."

He didn't look sorry. Not even the tiniest bit.

"How much longer is it going to take?"

"Hard to say. There are an awful lot of people to move, and we still won't have enough room for everyone. Are you absolutely sure I can't persuade you to look for pastures new?" He flashed me that smile of his which made me want to beat him around the head with a pogo stick. "I could probably improve a little on my last offer."

The man was a creep with a capital 'C'. He'd already tried to have the landlord throw me out, and now he was back to bribery. Well he knew what he could do with his money.

"I'm staying put. Now if you don't mind, I'd like to close the door so we can hear ourselves think." I edged him out, and then slammed the door in his face.

"Call me if you change your mind!" He shouted through the glass. There were so many spells I wanted to use on that man, but I wouldn't sink to Grandma's level— not yet, anyway.

***

Against my advice, Kathy had taken a part-time job working for Grandma at Ever A Wool Moment. She would often call around at my office during her lunch break—just for a chinwag, according to her. To scrounge a free coffee and custard creams more like.

"What on earth is going on out there?" she said.

"It's Armitage. They're moving in."

"The solicitors? I thought you told him to sling his hook?"

"I did, but the other occupants of this building took his money and moved out. I'm the only one holding out."

"I bet he loves you."

"Grandma was around here earlier." I smiled. "She wasn't happy."

"About Trading Standards?"

"She thinks I reported her."

"Why would she think that?"

I shrugged. "Me and her just don't seem to have hit it off." I could hardly tell Kathy about my suspicions that Everlasting Wool owed much to magic.

"I have news!" Kathy grinned ear to ear.

"Are you pregnant again?"

"No! Why would you say that?"

"No reason. I just thought maybe it was time for you to knock another one out."

"Knock another one—? No wonder you can't get yourself a man. Are you this romantic when you're out on a date?"

"I can do romantic."

Kathy shook her head. "Anyway, my news. I've got a promotion."

"Already? You've only been there five minutes."

"I know. Your grandmother obviously rates me highly."

"I'd settle for her not hating me. What's the promotion?"

"She's introducing another new line, and she wants me to head up the sales for it."

"What kind of line?"

"One-Size Knitting Needles."

"How's that work exactly? I thought they came in different diameters?"

"That's the great thing about these. They can be whatever size you want them to be. You just touch the needles to the pattern you're going to be using, and they adjust to the right size."

"Hang on. That doesn't sound possible."

"I know. It's like magic. According to your grandmother, it's a revolutionary new design which she came up with, and has patented. No one else can make them."

Unbelievable. How much more blatant could she be?

"So what does your new job entail?"

"I'm not sure exactly, but I get a ten per cent pay rise, so that's good. I really think you've misjudged your grandmother. She has a warm, generous side."

I laughed. "You keep thinking that." Right up to the point where she turns you into a cockroach.

My phone rang.

"It's Maxwell," I mouthed to Kathy.

She gave me a knowing smile.

"Hi, Jack," I said in my sweetest voice.

My good humour didn't last for long.

"Hold on, Jack, that's hardly fair."

I could tell Kathy was wondering what was wrong.

"I didn't mention it because I hadn't seen him then. I told him—"

The line was dead.

"What happened?" Kathy said.

"Jack Maxwell happened. The man is a complete asshat."

"Hang on. I thought you and he had made up."

"So did I, but it looks like we were wrong, apparently."

"What did he say?"

"I had a visit this morning from a young guy named Steve Lister. He's the boyfriend of the woman who's been kidnapped."

"Amanda Banks? I saw that on the news."

"He came in without an appointment to ask if I would take on the case. I told him I was too busy. I'm not, but I knew how sensitive Jack was about kidnappings after what happened with the Camberley case. I didn't want to risk ruining the working relationship we'd established, so I turned down the case."

"So why is Maxwell angry?"

"Because he heard that Steve Lister had been to see me, and he assumed that I'd agreed to take on the case. You heard—he didn't give me a chance to tell him I'd turned it down. Asshat!"

I stood up, walked through to the outer office, and had a word with Mrs V.

Back at my desk I punched the number she'd given me into my phone.

"Who are you ringing now?" Kathy said.

"Steve Lister. Who do you think?"

***

I was still spitting feathers long after Kathy had left. I'd managed to get hold of Steve Lister, and arranged for him to come in and see me the next morning. He'd been somewhat surprised to get my call, but I explained that I'd resolved a case early so was able to squeeze him in.

I couldn't focus on work because all I could think about was all of the things I wanted to do to Jack Maxwell. No! Not that kind of thing. My romantic interest in that man was over. I refused to date an asshat. Turn him into a rat? Maybe—I could get on board with that idea.

It was a beautiful afternoon, so I decided a walk might calm me down and clear my head. I deliberately headed in the opposite direction from Ever A Wool Moment. I couldn't handle Grandma and her stupid one-size fits all needles. Instead I headed out towards the common where I'd be able to sit on a bench and try to chill out.

So there I sat, minding my own business, and ignoring the ducks which had gathered around my legs. I was obviously sitting on the bench reserved for the professional duck feeders. You know the type: trainers, odd socks and a bag full of bread.

"Billy! Don't kick the ball near that lady." The woman's voice came from behind me. "Don't kick—"

The ball hit me on the back of the head with a thud.

"Sorry about that," she said, but she didn't look particularly sorry. "Boys will be boys."

I smiled and went back to ignoring the ducks.

"Billy! Be careful where you kick it."

Thud. Right on the back of the head again. Now, I realise that I have no parenting experience, but even I could see that little Billy was doing it deliberately.

"Billy. Be careful of the lady."

He'd *better* be careful.

Thud. Okay, enough was enough.

I picked up the ball and threw it towards darling Billy. As I did so I cast the 'move' spell which gave me control of the ball as it floated towards him. Billy had his arms stretched up in the air as he followed the ball's trajectory.

"Billy, be careful!" his mother yelled.

It was floating inches above his fingertips. So near, yet so far.

"Billy! Be careful of the—"

Splash!

Billy fell into the pond scattering the ducks in all directions. It wasn't deep, and within seconds his mother had waded in and pulled him out. The little angel was covered with mud and soaked to the skin. Shame. I waited until the ball was over the centre of the pond, and then let it drop into the water.

"Is he okay?" I shouted, doing my best to sound concerned. "Boys will be boys."

***

Curiously, I felt a whole lot better. The sound of Billy and his mother squelching their way out of the park had taken my mind off Maxwell. I was so over that man now it wasn't even funny. Just let him say one wrong word to me, and I'd set his butt on fire with a 'burn' spell. The Bugle regularly suggested that the police needed a fire lit under them. Well, I'd be more than happy to help with that.

My phone rang. If that was Maxwell coming back for more, I wouldn't be responsible for my actions.

"Jill!" Pearl screamed down the phone. "It's Pearl."

"And Amber."

"Let me do the talking," Pearl said.

"Why? She's my cousin too."

"Girls, what's wrong?"

I could tell by their voices that all was not well.

"Miles Best!" Amber yelled.

"We're going to kill him!"

Miles Best had been at school with the twins. They'd both secretly had a crush on him, and had been hoping to rekindle the flame at a recent school reunion. Needless to say their fiancés had been unaware of all this. Anyway, as it turned out, the years had not been kind to Miles Best, and neither of the twins was now interested in him. He hadn't taken 'no' for an answer until I'd stepped in and warned him off. I had thought that was an end to the matter, but apparently not.

"Is he stalking you again?"

"No. Much worse than that. It's his shop."

"What's his shop?"

"The new cake shop across the road from Cuppy C. It's his shop."

"Best Cakes is Miles Best? Are you sure? Have you spoken to him?"

"No, but we saw him, and that new girlfriend of his, in there today. It has to be his shop. What are we going to do, Jill?"

"Don't panic. I'm coming over tomorrow. We can talk about it then."

Chapter 7

Steve Lister was waiting for me when I arrived at the office. Stony-faced he seemed to have aged even from the day before.

"Have you been waiting long?"

"Not long. Thank you for agreeing to take on the case. I didn't know what I was going to do."

"No problem. I hope I'll be able to help. Let's go through to my office."

"Jill!" Mrs V called after me. "You haven't forgotten that Donald is taking me out for lunch today, have you?"

"Of course not. I'm looking forward to meeting him."

She frowned. "You won't say anything stupid to him, will you?"

"Me? Why would I?"

"I know you think you're funny, but people don't like to have their names made fun of."

"I promise to be on my best behaviour."

Such promising material too. Seriously, what kind of parents with the surname 'Hook' would come up with the name Donald? Surely they must have foreseen the consequences. Had they never watched cartoons?

"Thanks again, Miss Gooder," Steve Lister said.

"Call me Jill, please. Obviously I've seen the news reports, but it would probably be best if you brought me up to date with events as you know them."

That didn't take long. It turned out that he didn't know much more about the actual kidnapping than had been reported in the press.

"What about Amanda's parents?"

"They won't even speak to me."

"Why not? Did you fall out with them or something?"

"They've never liked me — right from the get-go. They didn't think I was good enough for Amanda. They were right in some respects, but they could see she was in love, so they were forced to tolerate me. Since she was abducted, they've refused point blank to speak to me. They won't let me in their house. They basically refuse to acknowledge my existence."

I could see that he was barely holding it together. Didn't Amanda's parents understand that he was hurting just as much as they were?

"Where was she snatched?"

"No one saw her being taken. The first anyone knew about it was when someone found the note."

"The ransom note?"

"No. There hasn't actually been a ransom request as such."

"How can you be sure if her parents won't talk to you?"

"They're divorced. Her mother remarried — a man called Bob Dale. He's a fantastic guy — more of a parent to Amanda than her birth parents have ever been. He and I get on great too. He's been keeping me posted."

"You mentioned a note?"

"Yeah. Like I said, it wasn't really a ransom note. It said something like: 'We have Amanda. Don't call the police or she will die. We will be in touch'."

"But they haven't? As far as you know?"

"No. Bob would have told me. Is that unusual?"

"I'm not sure." I was no expert when it came to kidnapping. I had no doubt that Jack Maxwell would know, but I could hardly ask him. "What are the police doing?"

"Not much. They say they are, but nothing seems to be happening. They talked to me a couple of times, but I couldn't tell them anything. I think everyone is waiting for the ransom note to arrive." He wiped away a tear. "Do you think she's still alive?"

I had no idea. "I'm sure she is. Whoever has got her is in it for the money. They have to keep her safe if they want to get paid."

"It doesn't always work out like that though, does it?"

"What do you mean?"

"Look at the Camberley kidnapping. The ransom got paid and they still killed her."

"That isn't going to happen here," I said with as much conviction as I could muster.

Maybe I'd been too rash in deciding to take on this case. Maxwell had been an asshat on the phone, but it was understandable given what had happened in his previous kidnapping case. I should have kept my cool and stayed out of it, but how could I back out now that I'd built up Steve Lister's hopes?

"I need to speak to Bob Dale," I said. "Can you arrange that? Do you think he'll talk to me?"

"He definitely will. I'll sort something out and either he or I will give you a call."

***

I was just starting to feel peckish when I heard a man's voice in the outer office.

"You must be Jill. Annabel has told me so much about you. It's a pleasure to meet you. My name is Donald—"

Please don't say it. I'll never be able to keep a straight face if you do. Mrs V was looking daggers at me.

"Donald Hook."

I grabbed a tissue from my pocket and pretended to sneeze. It was the only way I could stifle the laugh.

"Sorry about that," I said.

Mrs V's face reddened with anger. Oh dear, I was in for it later.

"Pleased to meet you," I said. "I hear you and Mrs V – I mean Annabel, go way back."

"We do indeed. We were something of a 'thing' back in the day. Weren't we Annabel?"

Mrs V giggled like a young school girl. This was definitely a side of her I hadn't seen before.

"Did she knit back then?" I figured small talk might take my mind off his name.

"Knit? Annabel?" He laughed. "No, she was quite the wild child."

"Really? Tell me more."

Mrs V grabbed Donald's arm. "No time for that now. We'll be late for our reservation."

"Oh, okay," Donald said, as he was dragged to the door. "Nice to meet you, Jill."

"You too. See you later, Wild Child."

***

I didn't feel like driving, so I used magic to transport myself to Candlefield. I misjudged the spell a little, and landed on the next street to Cuppy C. As I turned the corner, I immediately knew this was not going to be a good day. The queue outside Best Cakes stretched half way down the street.

"Have you seen that?" Amber yelled at me as soon as I walked through the door. I was the only person in the cake shop.

"How's the tea room doing?" I said.

"The tea room's okay—for now. But how long will it be before that snake across the road decides to open one of those too?"

"Where's Pearl?"

"She's gone upstairs for a lie down. She's got herself all worked up. What are we going to do, Jill?"

"It's too early to start panicking. It's his opening day— he'll have lots of silly offers that he won't be able to maintain. Give it a week and see how things are then."

"But what if no one wants our cakes any more?" Pearl had appeared, red-eyed at my side.

"Are you okay?" I put an arm around her shoulder.

"Cuppy C is our baby. It means everything to us. What will we do if Miles Best drives us out of business?"

"I think you two are over-reacting a little." Something I was never guilty of—obviously. "You have first mover advantage."

Listen at me with my *'first mover advantage'*. I'll be *'blue-sky thinking'* next.

"Once Miles' opening sale is over, you'll see business pick up again."

"I hope you're right." Pearl sniffed. "I couldn't bear it if I had to go and work for someone else."

"I do have one suggestion," I said. "But I'm not sure you're going to like it."

"Any ideas would be welcome," Amber said.

"You should ask Grandma for help."

"Any ideas *except* that one."

"Hear me out."

"Grandma?"

"Look, you know that I'm no fan of Grandma, and there's no love lost between us, but you should see what she's achieved with Ever A Wool Moment. That place has only been open for five minutes, and it's going from strength to strength. It pains me to admit it, but the woman is a marketing genius. That shop of hers is always full. She must be making more money in a month than I make all year. There isn't a week goes by that there isn't some new marketing initiative. You should ask her to help you."

"But—but—it's Grandma."

"Isn't there something else we could do instead?" Pearl sounded desperate.

"You could offer up a prayer, but I'm not sure that would be as effective. You have to bite the bullet, and ask her."

"Will you do it?" Amber said. "Ask Grandma, I mean."

"Me?" I laughed. "She hates me. She came to my office a couple of days ago, and accused me of setting Trading Standards on her."

"Did you?" Pearl asked in all seriousness.

"No! Of course I didn't. I'm not her biggest fan, but I wouldn't do anything like that."

Not strictly true—I had considered reporting her for using magic for financial gain in the human world, but there was no reason to tell the twins that.

"Please, Jill!" Amber said. "You're much better at this kind of thing than we are. You're not scared of her."

"Okay. I'll have a word, but don't blame me if she says

no."

***

Cuppy C was so quiet that the twins left the staff in charge while we all went to Aunt Lucy's.

"Jill's right," Aunt Lucy said. "It's too early to panic yet. Wait until the dust settles and then see how things are."

I was pleased to see that Lester was at Aunt Lucy's house. They'd recently become an item, but there was a brief hiccup when Lester had discovered that he'd lost his magic powers. He was so embarrassed that he'd been avoiding her. I'd been able to help by putting him in touch with Annie Christy, who was involved with SupAid, a charity which helped sups who lost their powers.

I waited until I got Aunt Lucy alone, and then asked her about Lester.

"Things are much better, dear. Thanks to you and Annie Christy. The specialist she put Lester in touch with has worked wonders."

"Does he have his powers back?"

"Not yet. It's going to be a long job according to the specialist, but there are no physical reasons why he shouldn't make a full recovery in time. We just have to be patient."

"Nonsense." Grandma did her usual trick of appearing out of nowhere. "I assume we're discussing Fester?"

Aunt Lucy's face flushed red, and I thought for a moment she was going to launch the rolling pin at Grandma.

"His *name* is *Lester*, as you well know. And yes, we are discussing his rehabilitation."

"What's wrong with him?"

"He has temporarily lost his powers—you know that."

"Do you know what you call a wizard with no magical powers?" Grandma said, and then paused a moment for dramatic effect. "A human."

"Mother!" Aunt Lucy lunged for Grandma who disappeared before our eyes. "I'll swing for that woman one day."

"I'm sure she didn't mean it."

"Oh, she meant it. And I'll mean it too when I strangle her."

Needless to say, we were all incredibly disappointed when Grandma sent word that she wouldn't be joining us for dinner.

"After all I do for that woman," Aunt Lucy said. "No one else would see to her bunions."

"Mum!" Pearl screwed up her face.

"Gross, Mum. We're eating," Amber said.

"Sorry girls. Sorry everyone. It's just that she drives me to distraction. She never has a good word for anyone. If I ever get like that, I want you to shoot me."

"Don't worry, I will." Amber laughed.

"You'll have to get there before me," Pearl said.

Chapter 8

I didn't need to ask Mrs V how her lunch date with The Captain went. She'd done nothing but smile and talk about him since then. I should have been pleased for her—I *was* pleased for her—but I still had a nagging doubt. There was something about The Captain that didn't ring true to me.

"When will you be seeing The Captain again?" I enquired.

"I do wish you wouldn't call him that. It's rather puerile."

Rather harsh—a bit childish maybe, but not puerile.

"Sorry. Just my silly joke. When will you be seeing Don again?"

"His name is Donald. He doesn't like to be called Don. I saw him last night actually. He made me a proposition."

"Mrs V! It was only your second date."

"Not that kind of proposition. Really, Jill, your mind could do with a good scrub."

"Sorry, I just—I thought—I'll shut up."

"That's the best idea you've had for a while."

Ouch.

"Donald thinks we should buy a property together."

"What? Like live together? Wouldn't it be easier for him to move in with you?"

"There you go again—jumping to conclusions. It would be an investment opportunity."

What was that I could smell? A rat maybe?

"Donald says property in Europe is the best investment there is at the moment."

"Where in Europe, exactly?"

"I don't recall. I think it began with an 'N'."

"Never-never land?"

She gave me a look. I really should have known better because she had a knitting needle in her hand.

"Isn't it a little early to be jumping into any kind of business venture with him? After all, he only reappeared a few days ago."

"Donald says we have to move quickly or we'll miss the boat."

I just bet he did. "I see."

The smell of rat was getting stronger and stronger. Maybe it was time for me to take a closer look at The Captain.

"There's a parcel." Mrs V fished a small box-shaped package out of her drawer. "It's addressed to the cat."

"To Winky?"

"Do you have more than one cat in there?"

This wasn't the first time Winky had received mail. A short while ago he'd been selling Mrs V's scarves (unbeknown to her), and using the proceeds to buy himself treats. What kind of scam was he running this time?

"Is that for me?" Winky jumped down off my chair and slid across the room. It was ages since I'd seen him wearing the little socks, which Mrs V had knitted for him.

"What are you up to?" I said.

"I'm not up to anything, and I'm disappointed you would think I am."

He did 'hurt' so well, but it didn't have me fooled.

"What is it then?" I shook the parcel.

"Careful! You might break it. Open it if you like. I have

nothing to hide."

I called his bluff, and ripped open the package.

"It's a smartphone." I read the card. "From Bella."

"Yes!" He punched the air. "She said she was going to buy one for me."

"Why would she buy you a smartphone?"

"Because *you're* too tight to buy one for me."

"That's not what I meant. And what do you mean 'tight'? I'm not tight. I'm just careful."

"That's what all tight people say. Now, are you going to give it to me or what?"

"They're a bit complicated." I passed it to him. "You might need me to help—"

He whizzed through menus and set-up screens, logging into the Wi-Fi (how did he know the password?), and was soon downloading apps like a pro.

"Where did you learn how to do all that?" It had taken hours of tuition from Peter for me to get up to speed on mine.

"What's to learn? It's simple."

"How do you even manage to hold it? You don't have opposable thumbs."

"Opposable thumbs?" He sneered. "You humans."

"Hey, who are you calling human?"

"Humans, sups—all the same to me. You're all so taken up with your fancy opposable thumbs." He put on a stupid high-pitched voice. "Look at me with my opposable thumbs. I'm so superior. Blah, blah, blah."

"Who was that meant to be an impression of?"

"You of course."

"I don't sound anything like that."

"Anyway, as I was saying," he continued. "Opposable

thumbs — highly overrated. All you need is a little hand eye coordination and the skillz."

"Skillz?"

"Yeah. Skillz like what I got."

"Who's paying the tariff on the phone?"

"Don't worry. Bella is going to keep it topped up for me. She's making a fortune from her modelling."

My cat, Winky — the kept man.

***

At his request I met Bob Dale, Amanda Banks' stepfather, at a small diner just outside Washbridge. I arrived five minutes early, but he was already waiting for me in his car — a Bentley with a personalised number plate. I didn't know much about Bob Dale other than that he was wealthy. The little research I'd had time to do revealed he'd built up and then sold a software company before the age of thirty. It hadn't surprised me to learn he was rich. From what I'd heard, his wife Patty, formerly Patty Banks, liked her men wealthy. Although the terms of her divorce settlement had remained secret it was rumoured that she'd walked away with a shade under ten million when her marriage to Amanda's father had ended.

"Jill?" Bob Dale looked more like a cowboy than a software geek. He was wearing jeans, and a white shirt, open at the collar.

"Thanks for meeting with me."

"No problem. Anything that might help to get Amanda back is fine by me. Shall we go inside?"

Bob bought the drinks, and we found a quiet corner at the back of the diner.

"How do you want to play this?" he said.

"Let's start with Amanda. How close are you to her?"

"We're very close. I don't have children of my own. My first marriage ended after only a couple of years—too young—both of us. When Patty and I got together, I wasn't sure how Amanda would react to me. I was afraid she might think I was trying to take the place of her father. I needn't have worried—we seemed to hit it off straight away. She's actually told me that she feels able to talk to me more than she ever has to her father or her mother. Patty isn't what you'd call the nurturing type. And Dexter—" he hesitated. "Honestly, Dexter Banks is not a nice man."

"How do you and he get along?"

"We don't. I've tried to reach out to him, but he doesn't want to know. I suppose I can't blame the man. I have his wife and I'm much closer to his daughter than he ever was. Let's just say I'm not his favourite person."

"What about Steve?"

"Steve's a great guy. I liked him from the get-go. And even if I hadn't, it wouldn't have mattered. Amanda is mad about him, and he's mad about her."

"What do her parents think of Steve?"

"Neither of them likes him. Patty does at least try to hide her disdain, but Dexter is outright hostile to him which of course has driven an even bigger wedge between him and Amanda."

"What can you tell me about the kidnapping?"

"Not much that you won't have already seen in the press, I guess. Dexter won't allow me in his house, so all of my information comes from Patty or the newspapers. The first I knew was when Steve rang me. He'd found a note in their flat."

"He mentioned that. Not a ransom note though?"

"No. It said something like: *'We have her, we'll be in touch'*."

"And since then? Nothing?"

"Nothing. At least as far as I know. It's possible Dexter has received a ransom note, but I think Patty would have told me."

"Is there anyone you can think of, anyone at all, who might be behind this?"

"Dexter has a high public profile. There must be any number of nut jobs out there who might do this to get at his money."

"What about friends? Do you know any of Amanda's friends?"

"A few by sight. She'd drop by the house with them occasionally. Her best friend is Rachel Nixon. They're very close—they have been since they were at school."

"You don't have a number for her, do you?"

"No. Sorry, but I believe she shares a flat in Washbridge city centre somewhere."

"No problem. I'll find her. Maybe Steve will have her number."

I couldn't help but wonder why Steve hadn't mentioned Rachel to me.

"Did you know Amanda had a part-time job?" Bob said.

"No. I thought she was at uni. I wouldn't have thought she needed the money."

"She wouldn't accept money from her parents or from me for that matter. She told Dexter what he could do with her allowance. She works in a small bar—bit of a dive actually. Bar Bravo, I think it's called."

Bob told me he'd be the one paying my fees, but he didn't want either Dexter or Patty to know I was working on the case. That suited me because I didn't want word getting back to Maxwell if I could avoid it. Bob promised to keep me posted if anything new came up, and I said I'd let him know if I made any progress.

I liked Bob Dale.

***

When I got back to the office, Mrs V was browsing through a number of glossy brochures. They appeared to be for timeshare properties. I was getting bad vibes about this, but I didn't want to risk upsetting her until I had more to go on. It was time to get my hooks into The Captain.

Winky was sitting on the sofa, tapping away on his smartphone.

"How come Bella decided to buy that for you?"

"Because she LOVES me."

"Hmm. I thought she found the semaphore more romantic?"

"She does, but all the flag waving was giving her muscles. That's a no-no for a cat model."

"Of course. Now you mention it that makes perfect sense."

"Do you mind?" He pulled away when I tried to look at the screen.

"What's that you're doing?"

"If you must know, I've just added my profile to FelineSocial.com."

"Is that like Facebook?"

"Yeah. They copied it."

"FelineSocial copied Facebook? Is that allowed?"

"No. Facebook got the idea from FelineSocial, obviously."

"Is Bella on there?"

"Of course. She's got almost two thousand licks."

"Don't you mean 'Likes'?"

"No, I don't. Likes are creepy. How would you feel if someone you didn't know came up to you in the street, and said *'I like you'*? You'd run a mile. And yet people do it on Facebook all the time."

"How is it better to 'lick' someone?"

"You're not a cat. You wouldn't understand."

"How many licks do you have?"

"None yet, but I've only just completed my profile. Bella will lick me soon."

She had better do or yours truly would never hear the end of it.

"What's that?" I pointed to Bella's profile.

"That's her status."

"Aloof? What's yours—Desperate?" I laughed.

He didn't. I was in the bad books again. Would I ever learn?

My phone rang.

"Jill?" Amber said.

"Hi."

"It's Amber."

"And Pearl."

"I'm talking if you don't mind," Amber said.

"I do mind." Pearl butted in. "I want to talk to her too."

"What is it girls?"

"We just wanted to tell you we've done the makeover for your neighbour."

"Mr Ivers? Great. How did it go?"

"I really like him," Amber said.

"He's boring!" Pearl shouted.

"He was not boring. He knows tons about movies."

"Like I said, boring."

"How did the makeover go?" I said. "Was he pleased with what you did?"

"I think so. We got him a new haircut, and a complete new wardrobe. He was a bit surprised at the cost though."

"That's great. Thanks for doing that guys. Look I have to go because the cat is giving me the evil eye."

"Huh?"

"Long story. I'll tell you later. See you soon. Thanks again."

Chapter 9

It wasn't difficult to track down Rachel Nixon. Just as Bob Dale had suggested, she shared a flat which was within walking distance of my office. I didn't have a phone number for her, and I didn't want to trouble her at university or at her place of work, so I figured an early morning visit to her flat might be my best option.

A young woman answered the door in a tee-shirt and boxer shorts. It looked like she'd only just crawled out of bed.

"Rachel Nixon?"

"No. She's in her room."

The young woman, who appeared to be nursing a hangover, ushered me inside and pointed to a door to the left.

I knocked.

"Just a minute."

The young woman who answered this door looked altogether more with it. She was dressed, and looked as though she was getting ready to leave.

"Rachel Nixon?"

"Yeah. Who are you?" Her tone was more curious than confrontational.

"My name is Jill—"

"It's the private investigator I told you about." The man's voice came from inside her room. Moments later, Steve Lister appeared at her shoulder.

"Hi," he said.

"Hi?" Finding him there had thrown me a little.

"I've told Rachel that I've asked you to investigate."

"Right. Good. You didn't mention Rachel when you

came to see me."

"Didn't I? Sorry. My head is so mixed up. I thought I had."

Steve was dressed. I wasn't sure if he'd been there all night or had arrived that morning.

"Do you have time to answer a few questions?" I asked Rachel.

"Sure. My first lecture isn't for another hour."

"Do you need me to stay?" Steve asked.

"No. I'd prefer to speak to Rachel alone."

"No problem." He gave Rachel a quick peck on the cheek, and said, "I'll call you later."

After he'd gone, I deliberately said nothing for a few seconds, hoping that Rachel might feel compelled to fill the silence.

"Do you think you can find Amanda?" she said, at last.

"I'm going to do my best. How well do you know Steve?"

"Steve and I hit it off from the moment he and Amanda started dating. He's a top guy — Amanda did good."

"Does he often come over?"

"Yeah. He and Amanda spend a lot of time here."

"Does that cause any friction with your flatmate?"

"No why would it? You met Carly, didn't you?"

"Yeah. She looked pretty hungover."

"She always is."

"So, have you and Amanda known each other a long time?"

"We went to school together. We were inseparable."

"If you don't mind me asking, is your family wealthy?"

"Wealthy enough to send me to a private school — that's where we became friends, but not rich like Amanda's family. That's what I liked about her. She never had any airs and graces. Never talked about the money or flaunted it like some of the kids did. She was—" Rachel caught herself. "I mean 'is'. She's my best friend. You *will* find her won't you? I couldn't bear it if anything happened to her."

***

I left more confused than when I'd arrived. Why hadn't Steve mentioned Rachel? Had he simply forgotten to tell me or was there more to their relationship than he was letting on? Neither of them had appeared the slightest bit awkward about being found together. Either it was completely innocent or they were both exceptional actors.

I was no further on than when Steve first came to see me. It all hinged on the ransom note, but so far there wasn't one. Or was there? Was it possible that the Banks' had received a note and had chosen, or been told by Maxwell, to keep it quiet—even from Bob Dale? I could always use magic to get inside the police station to see if they knew more than they were saying, but I didn't want to do anything that would risk antagonising Maxwell if I could avoid it.

The headline on the front page of the Bugle read, *'Is Amanda Dead?'*.

I resented handing my money to that loathsome rag, but I bit the bullet and bought the morning edition. It was, as I'd expected, up to their usual high standards. It was basically a rehash of the story which they had run twice already. There was no new information—they'd simply changed the angle. According to the Bugle the fact that no ransom note had been received wasn't good news, and probably meant that Amanda Banks was dead. Unfortunately, there was a good chance they could be right. The whole point of a kidnapping of this kind—one which involved a wealthy family—was to extort cash. The only reason I could come up with for no ransom demand being received was that Amanda had been killed— possibly while trying to escape. But even then I would have expected them to try to get some money from the family. It wouldn't be the first time that had happened. To have heard nothing at all, simply didn't make a lick of sense.

***

"Why do I have to go?" Barry could do 'pathetic' better than any dog I'd ever known.

"You'll learn things."

"Why do I need to go to an obedience class though? I'm not naughty, am I?"

Now I felt bad. "No you're not naughty—"

"Then why?"

"You can be a little boisterous at times."

"What does boy's truss mean?" Barry looked even more confused than he usually did.

"Boisterous. It means naughty," Grandma offered helpfully.

"Thanks."

"Don't mention it." She cackled then took her leave.

"See!" Barry whined. "You do think I'm naughty."

I needed to try a different tack.

"Do you like to go to the park?"

"The park! It's my favourite. I love to go to the park. Can we go now?"

"No. If you don't take the obedience classes, you won't be able to go to the park ever again."

"Why? That's not fair!"

"It's the new rules. All dogs have to go to obedience class or they won't be allowed in the park."

Barry sighed.

"What can I do?" I said. "My hands are tied." What? Don't judge. I'm allowed to lie if it's for his own good.

'No Bones About It' held classes in a large hall not far away from Cuppy C. There were ten of us in all: three witches, three vampires, two werewolves and two goblins. The dogs were a mix of breeds. A Rottweiler barked at Barry when he got a little too close to him.

"I don't like him," Barry said, cowering behind my legs.

"He's probably nervous. Don't get too close to him."

The woman who appeared through a door at the back of the hall would have given Grandma a run for her money in the ugly stakes. What? It's not my fault she looked liked she'd taken a tumble out of the ugly tree.

"Right then!" She barked. "Can I have quiet, please?"

Barry chose that moment to bark back at the Rottweiler.

"Barry! Shush!"

"Ladies, gentlemen and canines. Welcome to 'No Bones About It'. My name is Gretchen Bone."

I laughed—no one else did. I tried to cover it with a cough, but judging by the look on Gretchen Bone's face, I'd failed. Surely that couldn't be her real name?

"This is a ten week course. By the end of which, you

will have a dog which is obedient and a credit to you. That is of course if you follow my instructions to the letter. Do you all understand?"

Everyone, apart from me, said, "Yes, Ma'am."

Ma'am? Who called anyone Ma'am these days, and how come everyone else knew what to say when I didn't?

"What's your name?" she shouted at someone.

"I said, what's your name?" she shouted even louder.

Oh bum! The Bone was talking to me.

"What's *my* name?"

"You do know your name, I assume?"

"Sorry, yes. I didn't know if you meant my name or the dog's."

"I'm looking at you, aren't I?"

"Sorry. It's Jill. Jill Gooder."

"Oh, you're that new witch, aren't you?"

"Err—yes."

"Well, Jill Gooder. Did you receive the letter which I send out to all those who enrol on the course?"

"Yes."

"And did you read it?"

"Err—yes."

"All of it?"

"Err—I think so." I'd looked at it to find out the date and time of the course, but I hadn't bothered to read the rest.

"If you had, then you'd know what I expect from those who attend my classes. Top of the list is that you address me as 'Ma'am' at all times."

"Oh, right. Sorry."

She glared at me.

"Sorry, Ma'am."

"That's better. I suggest that tonight you take the time to study the papers I sent to you."

"Yes, sorry. I will."

Another glare.

"Ma'am."

"It's good here, isn't it?" Barry whispered.

"Okay," The Bone said. "First of all, I'd like to see each of you walk with your dog on the lead. Try to get him to walk to heel."

"Did you hear that Barry?" I whispered.

"Walk to heel. Got it." He scratched his ear. "What's that mean again?"

I was the last to go. I was a little less anxious because several of the other dogs had failed to obey the command. The Bone had been quite understanding, and she'd reassured the owners that their dogs would be able to do it perfectly by the end of the course.

"Now you, Gooder." The Bone fixed me with her gaze. "What's your dog's name?"

"Barry."

"Barry?" She laughed, and everyone else joined in. Cheek!

"Right Gooder. Let's see how you and Barry do."

Much to my surprise and relief, Barry walked to heel perfectly. I was thrilled until The Bone began to yell. At me!

"You're walking much too quickly—slow down!"

"You're walking too slowly now—speed up."

"Longer paces!"

"Shorter paces!"

"Hold the lead higher."

"The lead is too loose!"

"Now it's too tight!"

By the time we'd completed the circuit, my head was spinning.

"Well done, Barry!" The Bone crouched down, rubbed Barry under the chin, and gave him a treat from her pocket. "You did very well—under the circumstances." Her gaze switched to me when she said the word 'circumstances'. "You, Gooder, on the other hand, have a long way to go."

"Right, sorry—err—Ma'am."

That pretty much set the tone for the rest of the session. The Bone would set us a task, Barry would do it perfectly, and The Bone would yell at me. By the end of the class all the other participants were giving me pitying looks.

"That was good!" Barry said, as we walked back to Cuppy C. "I like Mrs Bone—she gave me treats. When can we go again?"

"We are never setting foot in that place ever again."

"But you said—"

"Shush, and be obedient."

Chapter 10

When I saw I had a voicemail from Bob Dale, I assumed it would be about the Bugle's article. I was wrong. When I called him back, he had much more significant news. A ransom note had been received. Except that he didn't use the word *'received'*. Instead, he said the note had been *'found'*.

"So no one saw who delivered the note?" I said.

Bob was riding one of his horses when I rang. He was in the countryside somewhere, and the reception on his phone was patchy.

"No. Dexter Banks found the note. I'm not sure of the details yet, but I know no one saw it being delivered."

"How come he told you anyway? I thought you and he weren't on speaking terms? Did your wife tell you?"

"No. It was Dexter himself, but there's a reason for that. The note specifies that I must be the one to deliver the ransom."

"Any idea why they asked for you?"

"No, but I'm happy to do it if it gets Amanda back."

"What about the money?"

"The money isn't a problem for Dexter. He's had a huge amount on standby ever since he knew Amanda had been kidnapped."

"What do the police have to say?"

"They're happy for me to make the drop. They're going to follow me."

"What does Dexter think about that?"

"He seems remarkably relaxed about it. I thought he'd object to them following, but he seems okay with it."

"When is the drop?"

"Sunday."

"How will they let you know where to take it?"

"I already know. The note specified where the money was to be dropped."

That made no sense. The kidnappers must have realised that would give the police time to set up surveillance around the area, and to plan how best to seal it off once the cash had been collected. Either the kidnappers were rank amateurs or they were ultra smart and I was missing something.

"I'll follow you too," I said.

"Okay, but don't let the police spot you. The guy in charge asked if the family had brought anyone else in."

"Jack Maxwell?"

"Yeah. That's him. We told him no one else was involved."

"Good. What about Steve? Does he know about the ransom note?"

"He does, but only because I told him. Dexter and Patty wouldn't have bothered."

***

I'd asked Grandma if she'd give the twins the benefit of her marketing expertise to help them compete with the new cake shop. As I'd expected, she'd given me a hard time, and had wanted to know why she should bother. After a major charm offensive — okay I crawled, begged and pleaded — she finally agreed to give them a few minutes of her precious time. I hoped the twins appreciated the sacrifice I'd had to make. I suppose I should have been grateful I hadn't had to tend to her bunions as part of the deal.

"How did the dog obedience classes go?" Pearl grinned. Something told me Barry had been talking behind my back.

"Okay, thanks."

"That's good." Amber was grinning all over her face. "Because we have a 'bone' to pick with you."

"You two have been talking to Barry, haven't you?"

"You have to admit it's funny." Pearl giggled. "It sounds like you're the one who needs training."

"That woman didn't know what she was talking about. I won't be going back."

"Ahh. Poor Barry." Amber smirked.

"Never mind Barry. How's the cake shop doing? Still struggling with the competition?" I gestured across the road.

"Business has picked up a little," Pearl said, more serious now. "But it's still only at about sixty percent of what it was before *that* creep opened his shop." She scowled, and I turned to see Miles Best staring back at her—he had a huge smile on his face. "He thinks he's so smart. I'd like to wipe that stupid grin off his face."

"Did you ask Grandma if she'd give us some marketing tips?" Amber said.

"I did. You two owe me big time. That's why I'm here this morning. She said she'd come over to get the marketing campaign rolling."

"Thanks, Jill. You're a saviour."

"Yeah, thanks Jill. By the way, how are things with you and Drake?"

"They aren't. I'm not sure what I should do about him."

Drake Tyson and I had seen each other a few times.

Nothing serious—not even what you might call an 'official' date. Then, just as things had started to look promising, I'd discovered he was a Rogue wizard who had been jailed for crimes committed in the human world. I'd dropped him unceremoniously only to discover from his brother, Raven, that Drake had actually been innocent all along. He'd been covering for his younger brother. I felt terrible for the way I'd treated him, but wasn't sure how to make it right or if I should just leave things as they were.

"You should get in touch with him," Amber said, once I'd brought them up to speed.

"I'm not sure. I didn't even give him a chance to put his side of the story."

"You have to try," Pearl said. "He's really hot."

"This is all very interesting I'm sure." Grandma barged her way past the three of us. "But if you put as much effort into running this shop, as you waste discussing silly boys, then you wouldn't need my help."

"Sorry, Grandma."

"Sorry."

"Right, well listen up. Today is the start of the Cuppy C marketing campaign. You'll be pleased to know that you'll be following a tried and tested methodology which has already proven successful in the launch of Ever A Wool Moment. So, are you ready to start?"

"Yes, Grandma," Amber and Pearl said in unison.

She snapped her fingers and suddenly her arms were full of—what? I wasn't exactly sure.

"These are costumes which I've had specially made." She held one of them up to show us.

"It's a cupcake," Amber said.

"It is indeed a cupcake. And these are 'twenty per cent off' leaflets."

"Who's going to wear those?" Pearl asked, but I had a feeling she already knew the answer.

"Who do you think?"

"Grandma," Pearl whined. "Everyone will take the mickey."

"No one will know it's you once you have them on."

"How do we see — or breathe?"

"There are tiny slots. Here look!"

"They look heavy."

"Stop your whining and get them on."

The twins looked to me for help.

I shrugged. "I think you'll look good in them." I couldn't suppress a laugh.

"I'm glad you think so, Jill," Grandma said. "Because I have three costumes."

Now it was the twins' turn to laugh.

It wasn't fair, and it wasn't funny. I'd had to grovel in order to persuade Grandma to help, but I would never have done it if I'd realised I'd have to dress up in that stupid costume.

"I can't breathe," I said.

"Stop complaining." Grandma waved her hand dismissively. "Breathing is overrated."

The three of us looked ridiculous. The bottom of the costume was so tight around our legs we could only waddle like penguins. The only saving grace was that Kathy wasn't there to see me.

"I've just taken a photo of the three of you to show to your sister." Grandma waved her camera in front of me.

Great! Kathy would never let me hear the end of it. Unless—I could always deny it was me. She'd never know.

"I took one earlier too," Grandma said. "When you were putting the costumes on."

"Thanks."

Out on the street, the three of us waddled up and down, handing out flyers and doing our best to ignore all of the snide comments. I noticed that Miles Best was standing outside his shop, and although he appeared to be laughing at us, I thought I saw a look of concern every now and then. Whatever my feelings about the costume, I couldn't deny that the flyers were doing the trick. There was a steady procession of people going into Cuppy C to buy the discounted cakes. The remaining staff had their work cut out to keep up with demand.

I spotted her when she was no more than a few yards away. I'd first met Alicia, aka Tess, in a park in Candlefield. She'd befriended me, and we'd met for coffee in Washbridge where she'd supposedly worked as a lawyer—that had turned out to be a lie. She'd poisoned me to try to keep me from competing in the Levels Competition. I could have died—not that she would have cared. I had no proof as yet, but had my suspicions that she was working for The Dark One or TDO as most people referred to him.

TDO was the most powerful of sups although his identity was unknown. He wanted me dead and had already made a number of attempts on my life. Quite recently, an ex-journalist who had claimed to have information on TDO had been found dead minutes before I was due to meet with him. He'd been murdered in Magpie Place. Shortly after that I'd received an anonymous card — on the front of which was a picture of a magpie standing in a pool of blood.

"Is that you in there, Jill?" Alicia said, her face only inches away from mine.

"What do *you* want?"

"I must say that costume suits you." She laughed. "And it saves us all from having to look at your ugly face."

Before I could respond, she pushed me over her outstretched leg. I lost my balance and the next thing I knew, I was rolling down the street.

"Help!"

I was rolling faster and faster; I was getting dizzier and dizzier.

"Help!" I hit the lamppost with a thud. "Ouch!"

Moments later, the twins who had abandoned their costumes, were helping me out of mine.

"She did it on purpose," Amber said, gesturing towards Alicia who was almost out of sight now.

"Are you okay?" Pearl took my hand.

"I'm fine. Just a little dizzy."

"That woman is a horror."

"Don't worry about her," I said. "I'll get my own back. Just see if I don't."

***

When the twins totalled the takings at the end of the day, they weren't just back to pre-Best Cakes levels, they were the highest single day of the year. Grandma, the marketing genius, had struck again. The twins drew up a rota which meant that they, and all their staff, would take turns to dress up in the cupcake costumes every day for the next week. I insisted that I'd really like to do my bit, but I had pressing business in Washbridge. I'm not sure they believed me, but they didn't push it.

"It's Mum's birthday next week." Amber took a bite out of one of the few remaining cakes.

"Aunt Lucy? How old is she?"

"Don't ask her that whatever you do." Pearl laughed. "She stopped having birthdays after she turned five hundred."

Aunt Lucy had explained to me that witches lived many times longer than humans. It was weird to think I could still be alive when Kathy's great, great, great, great, great, great grandchildren were born. "Is she having a party?"

"That's what we wanted to talk to you about."

"I don't like the sound of this."

"It's nothing to worry about. Amber and me thought we'd organise a surprise party for her."

"Are you sure? Will she like that?" Kathy had once organised one for me, and I'd hated every minute.

"She'll love it. Mum loves a good party."

"We've told Lester, and he's on board."

"So what do you need me to do?"

"We're all going to pretend we're busy on her birthday, so she doesn't think she's going to see any of us. We need you to come over and take her out while we set things up. When you come back we'll all be waiting for her."

"How am I meant to get her out of the house? Where should I take her? And what about Grandma?"

"What about her?" Amber polished off the last few crumbs.

"She'll let the cat out of the bag for sure. And, knowing her, she'll do it on purpose."

"We won't tell her," Pearl said.

"Have you forgotten she can read our minds?"

"We've already thought of that," Amber said. "And we have a cunning plan—ice cream!"

"Huh?"

"All of us have to agree that whenever we are in Grandma's company between now and the party, all we think about is ice cream."

"Why ice cream?" I asked.

"Why not? It's as good as anything. So remember, whenever Grandma is around, think about ice cream."

Chapter 11

The streets were deserted. Hardly surprising considering it was three am on a Sunday morning. Bob Dale had given me details of the drop he was going to make at six o'clock. It was to be at a disused railway bridge a few miles to the south of Washbridge. If I'd left it any later, the area would have been buzzing with police, but Bob had told me they planned to wait until just before the drop to throw a cordon around the area. In other words the plan was to allow the kidnapper to get to the drop off point, but then to snare him on his way out. The plan made sense and it worked in my favour because it allowed me to get close to the drop point before the police arrived in numbers. It was an area I knew well because my parents had taken Kathy and me there for picnics when we were kids.

I parked the car in a layby two miles away, and then made my way on foot. There was a keen frost which meant the ground was hard rather than muddy. By a little after four o'clock I was settled in a hollow beneath the roots of an ancient tree. I remembered it from my childhood—it had been one of my favourite hiding places when Kathy and me played hide and seek. From there I had an almost unrestricted view of the drop point which was below the bridge.

By six o'clock, my hands, toes, nose and ears were all numb with cold. I'd heard a few sounds—twigs cracking—that kind of thing. It could have been the police or it could just have been small animals. I heard the 4x4's engine when it was still some distance away. Two minutes later, it came to a halt under the bridge. Bob Dale climbed out, walked around to the passenger side, and took out a small, brown sports bag. After depositing the bag next to the wall, he got back into the vehicle and drove away. The whole thing took less than five minutes.

For the next hour, I never took my eyes off the bag. By the end of the second hour my legs were beginning to cramp, and it was becoming harder and harder to stay focussed. What was I doing there anyway? What exactly had I expected to achieve? When the kidnapper showed up the police would arrest him. Or should that be *if* the kidnapper showed up? Where was he?

Each hour dragged by more slowly than the one before. I was hungry and thirsty, and colder than I'd ever been. I must have started to nod off because I jumped at the sound of car engines. Two police vehicles pulled up close to the bridge. A uniformed officer got out of one of them, collected the bag, and then both vehicles were driven away. The drop-off must have been a bust. Maybe the kidnapper had spotted the police — who knew? Right then, I didn't much care — I just wanted to get home to a hot bath. I gave it another twenty minutes, and then climbed out of my hiding place. By the time I got back to my car and drove home, it would be almost midday.

I never saw or heard him coming. The first thing I knew was when I was flat on my chest with my arms behind my back.

"You're nicked," the police officer said, as he clamped the handcuffs on my wrists.

Before I knew it, another three officers had me surrounded. Two of them lifted me to my feet and dragged me to their car which was parked at the top of the embankment.

If I hadn't been so tired, I would probably have used magic to escape, but my brain was barely functioning and it was all I could do to stay awake.

***

The metal bench in the holding cell wasn't the most comfortable bed I've ever had, but it didn't stop me falling into a deep sleep.

"You never listen, do you?"

The words skipped around in my dream.

"Wake up!"

I opened one eye to see two legs inches from my face.

"What? Where am I?"

"Sit up!" Someone grabbed my hand and lifted me into a sitting position.

"Jack?"

"Detective Maxwell to you."

My brain kicked into gear and I remembered where I was and why. This wasn't good.

"What were you doing there?"

"Watching the drop."

"I know that, but I want to know why? I told you in no uncertain terms not to get involved."

"No one saw me."

"How can you know that? It's my guess the kidnapper did see you, and that's why he did a runner."

"He couldn't have. I was—"

"Save it for someone who cares. In fact, save it for the Banks family. You can tell your sorry story to them if anything happens to their daughter." With that he turned and walked out of the cell.

"Jack, wait!"

But he'd gone. A uniformed officer escorted me out of the police station.

Was Maxwell right? Could the kidnapper have spotted me? I'd been super careful, and arrived hours before the drop. But what if he'd already been there? What if he *had* seen me? What if something happened to Amanda Banks? Maxwell was right—I was an idiot. Why had I taken the case? The truth was I'd done it because I was annoyed at Maxwell for warning me off. It hadn't been about Steve Lister or Amanda Banks. It had been all about me and my stupid pride. If anything happened to Amanda, I'd never forgive myself. And Jack Maxwell wouldn't—that was for sure.

***

I collected my car from the layby, and then drove home. A hot bath and a change of clothes did nothing to lighten my mood. I'd messed up big time, and I had no idea how to put it right. The one thing I could do—had to do—was to tell Steve and Bob I could no longer work on the case. I'd done enough damage—I had to quit before it was too late—if it wasn't already.

I was about to leave the flat when my phone rang. It was Bob Dale. I braced myself for the tongue-lashing I knew I deserved.

"Jill, it's Bob."

"Bob, I'm sorry—"

"Listen. There were two notes."

"What?"

"The kidnapper left two ransom notes. Dexter was told to pass one to me, but not to mention the other one to anyone. While the police were watching my drop, Dexter made the real drop miles away."

"When did you find out?"

"Just now — Patty told me. She and Dexter are worried because the note said they'd get Amanda back within three hours, but there's still no sign of her."

"Do the police know?"

"They do now. Dexter told them about half an hour ago."

"Was the money collected?"

"Yes. Dexter went back to check. It was gone." Bob hesitated, and I could hear his voice waver. "What do you think this means? Is she dead?"

"No." I had no idea, but what else was I meant to say? "They've got their money. They have no reason to kill her."

"Who says they need a reason?"

I knew he was thinking about the Camberley case.

"What do we do now, Jill?"

We? I'd intended telling him I was no longer on the case, but how could I do that now? He was barely clinging on as it was.

"I'm not sure. Hopefully Amanda will turn up. In the meantime, I'll keep trying to find her."

"You'll let me know if you come up with anything?"

"Of course."

I should have felt relieved. The drop-off point had never been the bridge, so I couldn't have spooked the kidnapper. That seemed insignificant now. Where was Amanda, and why hadn't they released her now they had the money? I feared the worst.

***

I needed to clear my head; a trip to Candlefield was called for. The twins were busy in Cuppy C. Judging by the number of customers in the shop, their marketing push seemed to have done the trick. I gave them both a wave on my way up to my room.

"Barry? Where are you boy? Barry?"

It was unusual for him not to come running as soon as he heard my footsteps on the stairs. Maybe he was at Aunt Lucy's?

I was about to turn around and make my way over there when I spotted a handwritten note which had been left on my bedside cabinet. The note said Barry was at the BoundBall clubhouse. There was no name on the note to indicate who'd written it. Why would Barry be at the clubhouse, and who'd left the note?

I'd been to the clubhouse before when I'd helped to find the missing Candlefield Cup. The clubhouse was now shared by the vampire, werewolf and wizard teams. I tried the door, and discovered it was unlocked. As soon as I turned the handle, I could hear barking.

"Barry!" I held out my arms and braced myself as he threw himself at me. "How are you boy?"

Only then did I realise Barry wasn't alone. Another dog was standing a few yards away. His tail was wagging, but his ears were down as though he was unsure about me.

"Come here boy."

That was all the invitation he needed to approach me. I recognised him now. It was Chief, Drake Tyson's dog. I checked his collar tag just to be certain. Sure enough it read *'Chief'*.

What was going on?

Just then the door behind me opened, and in walked a familiar figure.

"Drake?"

"Jill?"

"This is not funny!" I yelled at him. "I was scared to death when I saw the note. If you'd wanted to see me, you should—"

"Hold on! I had nothing to do with this."

"Do you expect me to believe that?"

"Yes I do because it happens to be the truth. I found this in my hallway this morning." He held up a note that bore the same message as the one left for me. "What's going on?"

I shook my head, but I had a feeling I knew precisely what was going on. The twins had been quizzing me about Drake, and had tried to persuade me to get in touch with him. It looked to me like they'd decided to take matters into their own hands to orchestrate this meeting.

"It's nice to see you again." He smiled. Oh how I'd missed that smile.

"Yeah. Nice to see you too." I stared down at my feet. "I think I owe you an apology."

"No apology necessary."

I looked up, and met his gaze. "I should have given you an opportunity to tell your side of the story. I jumped to conclusions, and I shouldn't have done that."

"I guess you heard about my spell in prison?"

I nodded. "It was only when Raven explained what—"

"Hold on. You've spoken to my brother?"

"Yes. He caught up with me in the street and explained what had happened."

"When?"

"I don't remember exactly. Not long ago."

"Where?"

"Near the market place. Why?"

"I haven't seen him for weeks. He's disappeared, and I'm worried about him."

"I'm sorry, I had no idea or I would have let you know."

"It's okay. At least I know he was okay when you saw him."

"I could help you to find him if you like?"

"It's okay. It's my problem."

"I'd like to help. It would make me feel better about— you know."

"Okay, thanks."

Chapter 12

"But, we're busy, Jill," Pearl protested.

"Yeah, there's a queue in the tea room," Amber said.

I ignored their objections, and dragged them out of the shop, upstairs and into my room.

"What did you two think you were playing at?" I said.

They both looked at me with the same puzzled expression.

"Don't play innocent."

"I don't know what you're talking about," Pearl said.

"Me neither."

"I'm talking about this." I held up the handwritten note.

"What is it?"

"As if you don't know."

"Let us see."

I handed the note to Pearl. The two of them read it.

"We didn't do this," Pearl said.

"Yeah, that isn't our handwriting."

The twins were hopeless liars, so I knew they were telling the truth.

"I'm sorry. I was so sure it was you two. Then who was it?"

They both shrugged.

"Did you find Barry?" Amber asked.

"Yeah, he's fine. I dropped him off at Aunt Lucy's. Look, I'm sorry. I really thought you two had done this to try to get me and Drake back together."

"It's okay," Amber said. "I wish we had thought of doing something like that. How did it go? Did you kiss and make up?"

"There was no kissing involved."

"Pity." Pearl smiled.

"We did make up though. Or at least I apologised. I've agreed to help him search for his brother."

The twins hurried back down to the shop. I stared at the note. If it wasn't Drake, and it wasn't the twins, who was it?

***

I almost didn't recognise him when I got out of my car.

"What do you think?" Mr Ivers did a twirl for me.

"You look—great." And the weird thing was—I wasn't lying. I felt even worse now about having wrongly accused the twins. They'd done an incredible job on Mr Ivers. His hair was shorter and suited him much better. But it was the clothes which made the man. He looked liked he'd recently finished a fashion shoot for one of the more hip men's retailers. If he wasn't such a bore, I'd have fancied him myself.

"Please thank Amber and Pearl for me. They were great."

"I will."

"They have boyfriends, I guess?"

"They're both engaged."

"Pity. Still, now I have my own newspaper column and my new look, the girls should come flocking."

"Yeah, you'll have to fight them off." Or talk to them about movies for half an hour—that would do the trick.

***

The next morning, I sold my soul once again by buying

a copy of the Bugle. I was hoping for news on the kidnapping, but there was nothing—not even a mention. At this stage, no news was probably bad news. I called Steve and Bob. Neither of them had heard anything. Bob did tell me Dexter was losing patience with the police, and had threatened to employ a P.I. himself. That would have gone down well with Maxwell. Speaking of whom, I wasn't sure if I should try to contact him. I felt like I should apologise for the other day, but what was the point? As soon as he knew I was still working the case, he wouldn't want to hear it. Perhaps it was best to let sleeping dogs lie.

***

Donald Hook was sitting next to Mrs V.

"Morning Mrs V, morning—Don—ald."

Mrs V glared at me. Donald barely acknowledged me. He was too busy working his way through the pile of brochures on Mrs V's desk.

"Look at this swimming pool, Annabel. Spectacular isn't it. And at that price, they're practically giving it away."

"It looks lovely, Donald, but isn't it rather hot there though. My skin burns so easily."

"That's what sun block is for silly."

I didn't like the way this was going, but I had a plan.

"Let me see," I said, as I walked around the desk. "I'm not sure the weather would suit you there, Mrs V."

Donald turned his head and gave me a look. I'm not sure he appreciated my contribution, but that was okay because while he was busy being annoyed, he didn't notice me slip a small tracking device into his pocket.

"Why don't we go down the road for coffee, Annabel?" Donald began to gather up the brochures.

"Oh, alright. Is that okay, Jill?"

"Sure. Knock yourselves out."

Mrs V and The Captain had no sooner left than the hammering started.

"What's that?" Winky looked up from his smartphone. He'd been preoccupied since Bella had bought it for him. I wasn't sure what he was up to exactly—probably FelineSocial and Angry Birds. Still, it made a change from listening to him complaining.

"Can't you make them stop?" he said. "It's giving me a headache."

He had a point. There was an almighty racket coming from somewhere outside. It sounded as though someone was hitting the wall with a sledgehammer.

"I'll go and check it out."

"Hurry up." Winky sighed. "I can feel a migraine coming on."

The scaffolding tower was directly in front of the building. A small crane was parked at the roadside, and was in the process of lifting a huge sign up to the men waiting at the top of the tower. I had to twist my neck to get a good view of the sign as it was being lifted into place: Armitage, Armitage, Armitage & Poole.

"Hold on!" I shouted to the men in the tower.

One of the men shrugged. He obviously couldn't hear me, so I ran back in the building, up the stairs and over to the window in my office.

"Oh, hello," the man in the tower said. He was directly below my window. "I couldn't hear you before."

"Where exactly are you fixing that?" I shouted.

"Keep it down," Winky said.

"Be quiet! I'm trying to sort it out."

"What?" The man looked puzzled.

"Not you, sorry. I was talking to—never mind. Where are you going to fix that sign?"

"Right here." He pointed to the wall in front of him.

"But it will obscure my little sign."

The man glanced at my sign, which was minuscule by comparison, and gave a shrug.

"That's our orders, sorry. You'll have to take it up with—" He read the sign. "One of the Armitage triplets."

Just what I needed—a comedian. "Don't worry. I will."

Gordon Armitage had a corner office the size of a football field.

"You didn't need to expand next door," I said. "You could have just moved the additional staff in here with you."

"Good morning to you too, Jill. My P.A. didn't tell me you were here."

"I told her not to bother. I didn't want you to suddenly remember an urgent appointment elsewhere."

"What's so important that you had to see me right now? Have you decided to move out after all? I knew you'd see sense eventually."

"What do you think you're playing at with that sign?"

"I thought I heard drilling. Right on time—that's what I like to see."

"You can't put it there."

"I think you'll find I can."

"It's too big. It obscures mine."

"Really? Well that's unfortunate, but I have to say—I don't care."

"I'll take you to court."

He laughed. "Oh, Jill you're so funny. Have you forgotten what it is we do here? I'll give you a clue—we're lawyers. Please do take us to court. I'll tie you up in so much paperwork and red tape you won't have any time left to do whatever it is you do." He laughed again—louder this time. I was so tempted to turn him into a donkey or a piglet or—but I couldn't. I'd have to find another way to beat him.

Mrs V arrived back at the office just over an hour later.

"They're putting up a giant sign," she said.

"Yeah, I've seen it."

"Can't you stop them? No one will be able to see yours."

"I spoke to Armitage. He isn't playing ball, but I haven't given up yet. How did it go with whatshisname?"

She gave me a withering look.

"With Donald?"

"It's hard to make a decision. There are so many properties to choose from."

"Are you sure you have thought this through? I didn't think you liked to go abroad because of the heat."

"Donald says I shouldn't worry about that."

I bet he does. "You won't go making any rash decisions will you?"

"I'm not a fool, Jill."

Hmm.

***

I had some time before my dental appointment, so I thought I'd track The Captain for a while. Something about him just didn't feel right. Maybe it was because I was scared of him stealing my P.A. away, but it felt like more than that.

It didn't take me long to find him. He was in a small cocktail bar not far from Ever A Wool Moment. I'd crossed the road before I reached the wool shop because I didn't want to get waylaid by Grandma. The Liquid Lizard was a bar I hadn't been in before. It was in a basement, so there were no windows. It was dark, and seemed all the more so because it was so bright outside. I couldn't see The Captain, but the tracking device told me he was within a few metres. I grabbed a soda and followed the sound of voices. Sure enough, in a small booth at the far end of the bar was the man himself—he was sitting with a woman at least twenty years his junior. His daughter perhaps? Not judging by the way his hand was gliding up and down her arm. I went as close as I dared without being spotted, and then listened. It was hopeless. The awful music which was spewing out of the speakers meant it was impossible to hear what they were saying. It was time for the 'listen' spell. I tuned out all other background noises and focussed on their conversation.

Donald was all over the woman. She seemed less keen, and who could blame her.

"Did she sign the papers?" the woman said.

"No, but it's only a matter of time."

"You said that before."

"These things take time, Marigold."

Marigold? Really?

"I'm fed up of hanging around here." Marigold took a sip of her cocktail. "You know I hate the weather in this country."

"I know, but it'll be worth it."

"Are you sure she has the money?"

"Of course I am. She inherited it from her mother. Trust me, she has the cash."

"I hope you're right. I've got better things to do than hang around that seedy hotel while you play footsie with an old flame."

"She isn't an old flame. I told you, I wouldn't have even remembered her if I hadn't spotted her on TV. What would I have in common with some burnt out old has-been like that?"

How I resisted decking him, I'll never know. I'd heard enough. I knew there was something fishy about him, and now I had the proof.

Chapter 13

Evil. That was the only word for it. Tropical fish—I hated them. I'd been quite relaxed when I walked into the waiting room, but after watching them trying to eat one another for the last ten minutes, I was a gibbering wreck and I wasn't even in the dentist's chair yet. Still, it was only a check up. How bad could it be?

To make matters worse, the receptionist had informed me that my usual dentist was off ill, and I'd be seeing a locum.

"Jill Gooder!" A young dental nurse with perfect teeth called.

I followed her along the corridor, doing my best to forget about the fish.

"How are you today?" Perfect Teeth said.

"Fine thanks," I lied.

"You'll be seeing Ms Flowers today."

"Right, okay."

Hold on! Ms Flowers? It couldn't be. Could it?

"Daze?"

"Hi, Jill." Daze turned to Perfect Teeth and said, "It's okay. I won't need you for this one. Go take your break."

"You're a dentist now?" I couldn't hide my surprise.

Daze's real name was Daisy Flowers and she was a super sup. Her real job was to retrieve rogue sups from the human world. I'd already seen her working in a fast-food restaurant, in a launderette, and as a traffic warden—to name just three of her previous undercover guises, so I probably shouldn't have been so surprised. But I was.

"This isn't my favourite job." She gestured for me to get into the dentist's chair. "Staring at people's fillings and cavities isn't my idea of fun. Open wide."

"Hold on. Are you — err?"

"What?"

"Are you qualified to do this?"

"Of course. Now open wide."

"Wegerh asget."

"I can't tell what you're saying. Wait until I've finished my examination."

I winced as she caught a nerve.

"You need a couple of fillings, and you aren't flossing properly at the back. You'll need to make an appointment at reception for the fillings."

"Okay, thanks." I made to stand up.

"Wait. I wanted to speak to you actually. There's something you might be able to help me with."

I sat back down and listened.

***

When I arrived at work the next morning, it was the first time I'd seen Armitage's sign lit up. It was enormous, and just as I'd suspected, so bright you could barely see my poor little sign. Oh well, if he wanted to play dirty, he'd come to the right place. Game on. When casting spells, my focus was now so much better than it had been only weeks before. And I needed that focus if this was going to work. I checked there was no one around — it was still early — the rush hour hadn't started yet. I took aim, and used the 'lightning bolt' spell on first one letter, and then another until I had the desired result.

"Bed catch fire?" Winky greeted me when I walked into

my office.

"I'm allowed to come in early if I want to."

"I was having a fantastic dream." He sighed. "Me and Bella were on this water-bed and—"

"Stop! I don't want to know the sordid details. Anyway, how could you be on a water-bed? Wouldn't your claws—? Never mind."

"Anyhow." Winky scratched his ear with his back paw. "Now you're here, I want to take a selfie with you."

I hated selfies. I hated all photos of myself. I never looked like I thought I should.

"Why do you need a photo?"

"For FelineSocial."

"I'd rather not."

"Come on. All the other cats have a photo with their human."

"I'm not human."

"You're the closest I've got, so you'll have to do."

"What about Mrs V?"

"Are you kidding? I don't want my photo taken with that old battleaxe. Who's going to lick me then?"

"Okay. Just one then."

I was going to ask Winky where he'd got the selfie-stick from, but I thought better of it. Sometimes it was better to be blissfully ignorant.

We were sitting next to one another on the sofa. Winky was sporting a royal blue eye patch which he'd chosen especially for the photo. He had his front paws resting on my chest (those claws were sharp) so that we were almost touching noses.

"Say cheese!" he said.

Click.

"Look!" He held up the smartphone to show me the photo. I looked horrible.

"That looks nothing like me," I groaned.

"You're right. It does flatter you a little. Uploading it now." Winky did his magic with the phone. "There it is!"

I'd never had a Facebook account—I'd never really 'got' social media. But there I was, live on FelineSocial.

"It's under 'Pets'," I said. "I don't get that. If it's a web site for cats, why—?" Then the penny dropped. "Hold on. Does this mean I'm supposed to be *your* pet?"

"Of course it does. What did you think you were?"

What indeed?

I could hear Mrs V chuckling to herself as soon as she walked into the outer office.

"What's tickling you?"

"Morning, Jill. You're here early. I was just laughing at that sign. Haven't you seen it?"

"Can't say I noticed it."

"Most of the letters are out. It says, 'I Am Poo'." She burst out laughing again.

"Oh dear. That's most unfortunate." I grinned. "Gordon won't be pleased."

I waited until Mrs V was settled with her cup of tea before I spoke to her about The Captain. I knew she'd be devastated, but I also knew I had no choice but to let her know exactly what the slimeball was up to.

"Are you sure?" She wiped a tear from her eye.

"I wish I wasn't, but I heard every word they said."

"Who was the woman?"

"Her name's Marigold."

"Marigold? What kind of a name is that? How old was she?"

"Hard to say—she was wearing so much make-up, and the light wasn't good in there. I'd hazard a guess that she was twenty years younger than him."

"What does she see in him?"

"It certainly isn't his looks. It must be the money."

"If he has money, why come after what little I have?"

I'd wondered the same thing. "Maybe this is how he makes his money. He spotted you on TV, and thought you'd be an easy mark. Who knows?"

"Thank you, Jill."

"Don't thank me. I wish it had worked out differently. You deserve better."

"You're right, I do."

"What will you do now?"

"Don't worry about that. I'll take care of The Captain."

Kathy dropped by on her lunch break.

"Have you seen that sign outside?"

"Which one?"

"The 'I Am Poo' sign."

"Oh, that one." I laughed. "Good isn't it."

"What's it meant to be?"

"It belongs to my good friend, Gordon Armitage."

"The guy who wants to take over your offices?"

"That's the guy. Apparently he has a taste for poo. Who knew?"

"Anyway, it's high time you got your own sign sorted out," Kathy said.

"I will, I promise."

The sign outside still bore my late father's name: Ken Gooder. I didn't have the heart to get it changed, and besides it got the punters through the door. You'd be surprised how many people (read: men) didn't think a woman could do the job of a P.I. Then again, maybe you wouldn't be at all surprised. Men can be stupid.

Kathy seemed quite chipper which I found amazing. When Grandma had offered her a job in Ever A Wool Moment, I'd been sure it wouldn't last long. After all, who could work alongside Grandma, let alone *for* her? Grandma as a boss? It made me shudder just to think about it.

"How's the job?" I asked.

"Fantastic. The new product is flying off the shelves. I'm in line for a bonus this month."

Grandma was blatantly flaunting her magic—what with the Everlasting Wool, and now the One-Size Needles. I really ought to talk to Daze about her, but then I did kind of like living.

"What about Grandma? Doesn't she—? Isn't she—? I mean she must be difficult."

"She's the best boss I've ever had. Granted I haven't exactly had many. I think you're way too hard on her. Give her a chance, you might be surprised."

Not so much surprised—more amazed. The only explanation I could come up with was that Grandma was somehow using magic on Kathy to make her think she was enjoying the job, and to believe that Grandma was nice.

"Does she still think I set Trading Standards on her?"

"I don't think she cares about that now."

"How come?"

"They came around to do an inspection. A funny man with big feet and bad breath. I spoke to him first and I thought we were doomed for sure. A real 'jobsworth' if ever I saw one."

"So what happened?"

"Grandma had a quick word with him, and after that he was like a different man. Laughing and joking like he didn't have a care in the world. He only stayed half an hour. Said he was going to a pole dancing club, but he'd be giving us a clean bill of health. It was really weird."

Not all that weird to me. Grandma had obviously cast a spell on him, but I couldn't figure out which one. Then again, Grandma was a level six witch and knew far more spells than I did.

"What on earth is going on out there?" Kathy spun around in her chair.

In the outer office, Mrs V was shouting and, by the sound of it, throwing things.

"It's Mrs V and her ex-flame, Donald Hook."

"Donald — ?"

"Not duck, Hook. He's been trying to con Mrs V out of her savings. If he doesn't get out quick, she'll turn him into a pin cushion."

"But Annabel!" Hook shouted.

"Get out of my sight!"

"Ouch. That hurt. Ouch! Okay, okay. Ouch! I'm going. Ouch!"

Silence descended on the outer office.

"I hope she hasn't killed him." Kathy cringed.

"I hope he hasn't dripped blood all over the stairs," I said.

"Any news on the kidnapping?" Kathy asked. "The newspapers have gone very quiet on it."

"This is strictly between you and me, okay?"

"Of course."

"You mustn't tell *anyone*. Not even Peter."

"I promise."

"The ransom has been paid, but she hasn't been released. There's been no contact from the kidnappers since."

"Are you sure?"

"As far as I can be. I'm in touch with the boyfriend and the stepfather."

"That's terrible. I assume they fear the worst?"

I nodded. "And to top it all, I've really upset Maxwell."

"What did you do now?"

"It's complicated, but basically there were two ransom notes. The police and I followed the false trail; his men found me and threw me in a cell."

Kathy laughed.

"It's not funny."

"I know." She was still laughing. "What did Maxwell say?"

"I don't remember exactly, but he wasn't pleased."

"You've been here before. He'll get over it."

"Not this time. He was right. I shouldn't have got involved. I knew what had happened with the Camberley case, and still I had to stick my oar in. I should have left it alone."

"So, are you going to back off now?"

"I can't. I shouldn't have got involved, but now that I am, I can't just walk away from Steve and Bob. I have to keep trying. It's not like it can make things any worse between me and Maxwell."

***

Kathy had no sooner left than Winky began hissing at the wall.

"Mum?"

I knew by now that Winky could sense my mum's presence a few moments before she appeared to me.

"He doesn't get any better looking, that cat of yours," she said, as she appeared on the sofa.

"Maybe, but it doesn't seem to affect his love life."

"Poor Jill. Everyone is loved up except you. Even your cat."

"Thanks for the reminder."

"That's kind of why I'm here. To apologise."

"Apologise? For what?" Then it came to me. "No—you didn't. Please tell me you didn't."

"I did."

"Mum!"

"Drake seems like such a nice man, and I knew you were never going to contact him."

"So you stole our dogs?"

"Hardly stole. More 'relocated' them."

"How did you manage to move them?"

"I had help."

"Aunt Lucy?"

"You mustn't blame her. She said you'd be angry, but I managed to persuade her."

"You can't just stick your nose into my love life."

"There isn't really one to stick my nose into."

"Thanks for that."

"Anyway it worked out didn't it? You're back on speaking terms, aren't you?"

"Yes, but—"

"Then all's well that ends well. And now, I'd like you to do me a favour."

Unbelievable.

Chapter 14

"What's the favour?"

"Do you remember when I first tried to make myself visible to you?"

"Yeah. I thought I was going crazy."

"You were fighting it, so it took me several attempts to finally get through. You hid behind the sofa, do you remember?"

"I wasn't hiding behind it exactly."

"What were you doing?"

"I'd dropped something."

"Oh, right. Like you pretend to do every time a clown comes on TV?"

I hated clowns—they were evil, pure evil.

"And you expect me to do you a favour?"

"Sorry. Look, I have a friend who recently joined our ranks."

"Became a ghost you mean? Is she a witch too?"

"No, she's actually a human."

"So you can mix with human ghosts?"

"Yes, but sups still can't let on what they were when they were alive."

"So she thinks you are—were human?"

"That's right. Anyway, she's really upset because her daughter refuses to believe in ghosts, so my friend can't attach herself to her."

"What do you want me to do?"

"I need you to talk to my friend's daughter, and persuade her that ghosts really do exist."

"How am I meant to do that?"

"You'll think of something. I have every confidence in

you. I have her details here." She passed me a handwritten note. "Sorry again about the dog, but I'm sure you'll thank me one day. Oh, and by the way, what you did with the sign — very funny."

***

The next morning's Bugle had picked up the kidnapping story again. According to the article, the police were stepping up the search for Amanda. The depressing headline read: 'Time Running Out For Amanda'.

I gave Bob Dale a call.

"No one has heard anything." He sounded tired and resigned. "I'm trying to stay positive, but it's difficult not to fear the worst."

I wished I could offer him some crumbs of comfort, but I shared his fear. The question was: would it be better to find a body and have closure, or wonder for a lifetime what had happened to her?

On a much brighter note, I was in a meeting with my new accountant, Luther Stone. He'd taken over from my previous accountant, Robert Roberts, who had left the profession to work as a food critic. Luther was one of the best looking men I'd ever met. He looked more 'special forces' than 'bookkeeper,' but I wasn't complaining. Even though he'd told me my business needed only quarterly consultations, I'd signed up for monthly ones. So? Sue me. It was money well spent in my opinion.

"Jill?"

He'd apparently asked me something while I was

daydreaming about him, but I had no idea what. I'd been way too busy staring at those broad shoulders to listen to journal, balance, loss and profit stuff.

"Sorry?" I flashed him what I hoped was a sexy smile. Judging by the puzzled look on his face, I think I'd got it wrong again. I really should spend more time in front of the mirror trying to perfect that.

"I asked if you'd checked your overdraft recently?"

"Not recently. Do you work out, Luther?" What? I was just curious.

"Yes, several times a week."

I just bet he did. Now if I could just find out which gym he went to—

"Jill! The overdraft. Have you looked at it recently?"

"Yeah. Recently."

"How recently?"

"Oh, I don't know. Last week, month. Definitely within the last six months. Or so. Maybe last year."

"You're almost up to the limit."

"Really? Are you sure? I increased it."

"At the rate things are going, you'll run out of funds within the month."

"That's not good is it?"

"No. It's not. You need to increase sales and reduce expenses. You should consider moving to my new budget plan."

"What's that?"

"Instead of visiting your office, I conduct my consultation via Skype. Have you ever used Skype?"

"I've played around with it." An ex-boyfriend had a thing for it. It was a long and sordid story, and one I didn't intend to share with Luther.

"So should I sign you up for that?"

"Yes, please." The prospect of being able to get Luther on my computer at the touch of a button was too good an opportunity to pass up.

"Good. I'll sign you up and cancel the monthly visits."

"No!" I said way too quickly. "I mean, no, I want both. I find these monthly meetings are invaluable. If it wasn't for you coming today, I never would have known about the overdraft."

"You should have known. It's your job to know."

I'm a bad girl. Punish me. Punish me now.

"Jill? Are you okay? You'd gone again."

"Sorry. I've taken on more work recently. That money should be in the bank soon."

"Good. Well that's a start at least. But you still need to cut costs." He looked around. "Do you really need offices as large as these? They must be costing you a small fortune in rent. There's only you and the knitting lady—"

"And the cat."

"Of course. I'm sure you could make do with somewhere half the size, and half the cost. I noticed a new company has moved in downstairs. I'm not sure exactly what it is they do—err—the sign is kind of confusing. But maybe they would take over the lease on this place?"

"This was my father's office. I could never leave it."

"It's your decision obviously, but I recommend you give it serious consideration."

I promised I would.

"See you next month," I said as he stood up to leave.

"Yes. I'm moving to another flat soon. That might throw next month's schedule out a little. I'll contact your P.A. if I need to switch the dates around."

"Okay, bye."

He looked just as good from the back as he did from the front. Stop it, Jill. Stop torturing yourself.

***

I was getting into something of a routine now. I tried to practise magic for at least an hour, sometimes more, every evening. Originally it had been to make sure I could pass Grandma's tests, but it was more than that now. I wanted to be the best witch I could be. The twins appeared to be content to stay at level two. I wasn't criticising — maybe I'd have felt the same if I'd been brought up as a witch. But for me this was a new challenge, and I was determined to see how far I could go. Grandma was a level six witch; my mother had been one too. I owed it to myself and to my new family to try to emulate that achievement. Even though Grandma still scared me, I felt less apprehensive about the tests because I could see I was making progress.

I liked to get to the Spell-Range as often as I could because it was the best place to practise magic by far. When I'd first started going there, I'd tried to persuade the twins to join me, but they'd come up with all kinds of excuses. I'd soon realised they simply did not share my enthusiasm for magic, which was kind of weird. I'd got to know a few of the other regulars at the Range, including one level five witch who'd been very encouraging.

That day, I went to the Spell-Range with the intention of practising the 'shatter' spell. This was a classic example of a spell which was difficult to practise anywhere else. I asked one of the helpers who manned the Range to provide me with a suitable object to practise on. He in turn had asked what level I was. It took two of them to carry the stone statue, and place it on the ground in front of me. It looked expensive, but I guessed they probably bought these in bulk. I'd been surprised at the size of the statue—I'd been expecting something much smaller. Still, I was willing to give it a go. At least there wasn't anyone close by to see me fail miserably.

I'd honed my technique to the point where memorising and recalling the images came second nature. All of my energy now went on the focus. Grandma had stressed this time after time, and one day it was as if a light bulb had lit up. Much as I hated to admit it, she was right. It was the reason the twins were still stuck on level two, and probably always would be. Their level of focus was almost non-existent. I closed my eyes, whizzed through the images, and then focussed on the statue. Just as with the 'lightning bolt' spell, I had to direct the power by pointing at the object. I could feel the energy surge down my arm and out through my finger. The statue shook, but was still in one piece. I'd failed.

The force almost knocked me off my feet. The statue exploded into a trillion tiny particles which were taken by the wind. I'd done it. I wasn't sure why there had been that split second delay, but it had worked.

"They'll let anyone in here." The familiar, but unwelcome voice came from behind me.

I turned to see Alicia standing there. At her side stood the same skinny young wizard I'd seen with her before.

"Looks that way," I said.

"You should get back to the human world where you belong," skinny said.

"I still don't know your name," I said to him.

"Cyril."

"Cyril?" I laughed.

He didn't.

"Sorry. Cyril's a nice name. Oh, and while I remember, Alicia, thanks for tripping me up the other day outside of Cuppy C."

"Did I?" Alicia said. "I'm so sorry. I hadn't realised."

"Anyway, it's been nice talking to both of you, but I really must get on." I turned away.

"Don't turn your back on me!" Alicia spat the words, and at that moment I felt something sting the back of my leg.

I glanced down and saw what looked like a burn. That evil witch had used the 'burn' spell on me! This was something I'd never got around to discussing with Grandma or Aunt Lucy. I'd always assumed there was an unwritten law that a witch would not use magic against another witch. If such a law did exist, Alicia obviously didn't think it applied to her.

Another sting on my other leg made me jump to one side. Cyril was responsible for this one.

I didn't know what to do. I wasn't scared of them, but I was worried in case they were trying to provoke me into doing something which might have serious consequences for me.

"Stop right there, or I will wipe you off the face of Candlefield," Grandma shouted. She'd appeared directly between me and my two assailants. "Get out of here now, both of you, while you still can, or I'll make you wish you'd never been born."

Alicia scowled, but the two of them began to edge away.

"Can't you fight your own battles?" Alicia shouted back to me when she was some distance away.

"Why did you do that?" I turned on Grandma. "I could have handled those two."

"Maybe, maybe not, but it wouldn't look good for a relative newcomer to attack another witch."

"*She* attacked *me*."

"That's not how it would come out. Look, I know her mother and her grandmother. Alicia Dawes comes from a long line of wicked witches. Steer clear of her if you can. Otherwise things may get out of hand."

"Okay. Sorry."

"You did well with the 'shatter' spell."

"Not really. There was some kind of delay before it took effect."

"But then you *were* dealing with a level four object."

"Level four? No, that's not right. That was only a level two object."

"Do you doubt my word?"

"No, but I—"

"I had a word with the man who fetched it for you. I told him to give you the level four statue."

"Wow! So I did good didn't I?"

"You did okay. Like you said, there was a delay. It still needs work."

Had the statue really been for a level four witch? I found it hard to believe, so after Grandma had left, I caught up with one of the men who'd brought it to me.

"Excuse me."

"What can I do for you?"

"I was doing the 'shatter' spell earlier. I believe my

grandmother told you to give me a level four object?"

"Level four?" He shook his head. "No, that's not right."

I might have known. Grandma loved to mess with my head at every opportunity.

"That statue was for a level five."

Chapter 15

"Jill!"

I turned around to find Betty Longbottom hurrying after me. Betty, a tax inspector and sea-shell expert, had only recently moved into the block of flats where I lived.

"Morning, Betty."

"Morning." She was struggling for breath. "I'm glad I caught you."

I had a horrible feeling I wouldn't be.

"What's happened to Mr Ivers?" she asked, still breathing heavily.

"How do you mean?"

"He's changed. He looks—I don't know—different."

"Oh that. It's his new image. Suits him don't you think?"

"I almost didn't recognise him. Has he got a new job or something?"

"Not exactly. He's landed a weekly column on the Bugle. Movie reviews."

"Really? Who would want to read that rubbish?"

I shrugged. I could think of one person. "My cousins helped him with the makeover. He wanted a new image for his readership. Do you fancy him now?"

"Definitely not. He's so boring. I like my men to be men—if you know what I mean?" She blushed and giggled at the same time.

Maybe my initial impression of Betty had been wrong. Maybe she was something of a dark horse—another wild child, perhaps.

"Do you think the Bugle would be interested in a column on sea shells?"

"I'm not sure. I don't suppose it would hurt to ask. I wouldn't get your hopes up though."

"Incidentally, I've abandoned the idea of starting a newsletter," she said. "Sorry if I got your hopes up."

"Shame." Phew! "Oh well."

"I've decided to start a podcast instead."

"A podcast. On—?"

"Sea shells of course."

"Of course. Well, I hope it goes well."

"Actually, I wanted to ask you a favour."

Great!

"I need someone to interview me—for the first podcast. A kind of introduction, if you like. I wondered if you might do it?"

"Me? I don't know anything about podcasts."

"You wouldn't need to. I can sort out all the techie stuff. I just need you to ask me a series of questions."

"What kind of questions? I don't know anything about sea shells."

"Don't worry about that. I'll provide you with the questions—you just have to read them out. It will be just like being on the radio."

Except no one will be listening.

"I am quite busy," I said.

"Please, Jill. I wouldn't ask, but I haven't really got to know anyone else around here yet."

"What about the people you work with?"

She laughed. "They're much too boring."

Of course. "What about your friends?"

"I don't really have any friends."

Whoops.

"Except you of course."

"Me? Right, of course."

"So will you do it?" Her eyes pleaded with me.

"Sure. Why not?"

"Thanks. You're a good friend," she said, as she hugged me.

***

Winky pestered me for food and milk, but then went back to ignoring me once he'd finished both. He was totally engrossed in his smartphone. I tried to glance at the screen, but he covered it up.

"I hope you aren't watching something you shouldn't be watching," I said.

"Who do you think you are? My mother?"

"Well, yes. Kind of."

He laughed. "Anyway, people in glass houses and all that."

"What do you mean?"

"Do you understand how your web browser history works?"

"Of course." What on earth is a web browser history?

"Really? Are you sure about that?" He grinned. "If you do, then you'll know it's possible to see which web sites you've been browsing."

I didn't like where this was going.

"Hot accountants — need I say more?"

I could feel the colour rising in my cheeks. "That was — err — I was looking for — "

"It's okay. No need to explain. We all have our needs."

"No. It wasn't like that. I was trying to find a new accountant after Robert Roberts left."

"And he had to be hot?"

"That's an acronym. It stands for—err—Highly—err—Official—Tested."

"Highly, Official, Tested? What does that mean exactly?"

"You wouldn't understand. It's accountancy speak."

"And does it also require that they are bare chested?"

"Go back to what you're doing. Can't you see I'm busy?"

Memo to self. Find out how to erase my browser history.

***

Bob Dale called me, and I could tell instantly from his tone that something was wrong. I feared the worst.

"Steve has been arrested."

"What?" I hadn't been expecting that.

"What about Amanda?"

"Still no word."

"Why have they arrested him? Any idea?"

"I don't know. The police aren't telling me anything." His voice broke, and I sensed this was taking more of a toll on him than he'd care to admit. "There's no way Steve did this, Jill. He's a good guy."

"I need to speak to him. Does he have a lawyer?"

"Yes. I sorted out one for him as soon as I heard he'd been arrested. Arthur Greaves—he's one of the best. I'll speak to Arthur and see if they'll let you see Steve. I'll call you as soon as I have an answer."

"Okay, and Bob—"

"Yes?"

"It's all going to be alright."

"I hope so."

The police must have uncovered new evidence for them to have arrested Steve Lister. It was unlikely they'd found Amanda, dead or alive, because they wouldn't have been able to keep that under wraps. Bob Dale was unequivocal in his belief that Steve was innocent, but history was littered with cases where the person least likely to have committed the crime was eventually found guilty. Steve had seemed genuine enough to me, but then I had found him at Rachel Nixon's flat, and I still wasn't sure what if anything was going on between them.

***

"It's us!" Pearl and Amber yelled down the phone. I could tell by the echo that they had me on speakerphone.

"Hi, girls. How's things?"

"Good."

"Jill, we rang to remind you that it's Mum's birthday tomorrow."

"I hadn't forgotten. What's the plan?"

"We've got the food and drink organised, and we've contacted all of her friends. Everyone is coming."

"Does she suspect anything?"

"I don't think so. We told her we'll let her have our presents in the morning, but then we have to work all day in the shop, and then do stocktaking. Lester has said he has to work too."

"What about Grandma?"

They giggled.

"What?"

"It's so funny, Jill," Amber said. "We did what we said. Every time she's been in the room with us, we've thought about ice cream. She keeps chuntering on about young people eating too much ice cream."

"Hasn't she asked about Aunt Lucy's birthday?"

"Grandma?" Pearl laughed. "I doubt she'll even remember."

"Grandma doesn't do birthdays. Mum has to remind her of ours every year, and even then we rarely get a card."

"What do you need me to do then?"

"Keep Mum out of the house long enough for us to set everything up."

"How am I supposed to do that?"

"You'll think of something."

"What about Grandma?"

"We have that sorted." They laughed.

"Be careful. Remember what happened the last time you played a trick on her."

The twins had made the mistake of putting cake on the sofa arm while Grandma was asleep. She'd ended up with jam and cream all over her face. They'd ended up with donkey's ears.

"Don't worry. It'll be okay."

I hoped for their sake that it would. Crossing Grandma was not a good idea.

***

Steve Lister's lawyer, Arthur Greaves, got back to me just after midday. Steve was still being held, but Greaves had cleared it for me to accompany him to see his client.

"Where is he being held?"

"Still at Washbridge Police HQ at the moment. I'm trying to arrange bail before they ship him anywhere else."

"Will he get it?"

"Hard to say. The police are opposing it. They maintain he's a flight risk."

"Is he?"

"No. The only thing he talks about is Amanda, and getting her back. I've tried telling him that he needs to start worrying about himself, but it's like talking to a brick wall."

"Who's your contact at the police station?"

"Jack Maxwell. He seems okay. Do you know him?"

"Yes, we've met."

I had hoped Steve might have got bail or that he was being held somewhere else. I dreaded to think what Maxwell's reaction would be when he found out I was talking to the man he'd arrested. It was not going to be pretty.

I gave Aunt Lucy a call.

"Oh—hello, Jill."

She didn't sound her usual bubbly self.

"Are you okay, Aunt Lucy?"

"Me? Of course. I'm always okay."

She still didn't sound it.

"I'd like to come over to see you tomorrow. I want to bring your birthday card and present."

"That would be lovely." That seemed to have cheered her up a little. "What time?"

"Late morning or early afternoon probably. If that suits

you."

"That will be fine. I don't have anything planned. Lester and the twins both have to work."

I could hear the disappointment in her voice.

"Maybe we could take a walk somewhere together," I said. "I'd like you to give me the guided tour of Candlefield. I'm sure there's a lot I haven't seen yet. We could get tea."

"Not at Cuppy C. I fancy a change."

"Okay. You can choose. So, I'll see you tomorrow then?"

"See you then."

The twins' subterfuge had obviously worked. Now all I had to do was keep her out of the house, and hope Grandma didn't ruin things.

***

Much to my relief, I didn't encounter Maxwell on my way to the holding cell. The police officer told us we had an hour.

Steve's lawyer, Arthur Greaves, had brought me up to speed on the way over. Apparently the police had found a burner phone in Steve's locker at uni. There was a text message on it from Amanda. The message, dated just prior to her disappearance, asked him to meet her at her holiday home which was out in the country somewhere. The police had checked the house—they hadn't found Amanda, but they had found a bloody tee-shirt partially buried close by. Tests had shown it was Amanda's blood.

Greaves had been right. Steve Lister seemed almost unconcerned by his arrest. As soon as we walked in, he began to fire questions at us—all about Amanda. Only when we'd convinced him there was no news of his missing girlfriend was he prepared to answer my questions.

"Did you know about the phone?" I asked.

"I don't have another phone. The only one I have is the one I had on me when I was arrested."

"Any idea how it could have got into your locker?"

He shook his head. "It could have been anyone. The locks on those lockers are a joke."

"Why would Amanda send a message to a phone if it wasn't yours?"

"I have no idea. Are they sure it was from Amanda? Can't those things be faked?"

"The message definitely came from Amanda's phone."

"Then I have no idea. It makes no sense."

"The police said you don't have an alibi for the time when the message was sent."

"I was in bed—asleep."

"No one can vouch for that?"

"Like who? The only person who would have been there with me was Amanda."

I still had my concerns about Rachel Nixon, but this was not the time to air them, so I moved on. "What about the holiday home? Have you ever been there?"

"Yeah. Plenty of times. It was the one thing Amanda didn't mind accepting from her parents, but we'd only go when we knew they wouldn't be there."

"And you don't know anything about the tee-shirt?"

I saw the anger in his eyes. "What do you think I am? I would never hurt her. I love her. Have they confirmed it was Amanda's blood?"

"They're still running tests," I said, and drew a puzzled look from Greaves.

Steve didn't need to know it was Amanda's blood. If the police hadn't told him yet, there was no reason for me to do so. He was on the edge already—that might just push him over.

"It doesn't look good," I said, once we were out of the cell.

Greaves nodded. "If you could find out who planted the phone, that would help."

"Been to see your client?" Maxwell blocked our way. I hadn't seen him until he spoke.

"Detective Maxwell—" I said.

"Haven't you done enough damage?"

"I didn't spook the kidnapper," I said. "The drop-off at the bridge was just a decoy."

"Save it. We're done here."

With that, he stood aside and let us pass.

Chapter 16

When Betty had asked about the podcast interview, I hadn't realised she meant the next day.

"I have to go to a birthday party," I said when she knocked on my door.

"What time?"

"Around midday."

"That's okay then. It shouldn't take more than an hour."

"But—I—err."

"Thanks, Jill. You don't know how much this means to me. Here!" She thrust several sheets of paper into my hands.

"What's this?"

"It's a list of the questions I want you to ask me. Come on, everything is set up in my spare bedroom."

"I haven't even brushed my hair yet."

"Haven't you? I can't tell. Come on."

Betty's flat was white. Very white. I hardly dared step inside in case I left a mark on the white carpet.

"Come through. We're in here!"

The spare bedroom actually looked like a small recording studio. Tax inspectors must be well paid for her to be able to afford all of that kit.

"I didn't realise you needed all of this for a podcast."

"You don't really. A microphone and a laptop would probably have done the trick, but if you're going to do something, do it well."

Betty took control. I sat at one side of the white desk, she sat opposite me. There were two microphones—one for her and one for me.

"Right," she said, pressing keys on the laptop on the

desk in front of her. "I'll do the introduction, and then you can start the interview. Okay? Ready?"

I took a deep breath. "Ready as I'll ever be."

"Remember to speak clearly."

I gave her the thumbs up.

"Welcome to Betty's Sea Shell Podcast. I'm Betty Longbottom, and I'll be your host every week. For this first edition I've invited Jill Gooder, a local celebrity, to interview me."

Betty pointed to me and mouthed the words, "You're on."

Local celebrity, eh? I was beginning to warm to this.

"Betty Longbottom. Why don't you start by telling the listeners how you became interested in sea shells?"

"Thank you, Jill. That's a very interesting story."

It wasn't. Trust me on that one. It was, however, a very long story. So long, I'd almost nodded off by the time I realised she'd finished, and was waiting for the next question.

"Thank you for that Betty. Very interesting." What? I was reading from the script. "What are your top ten favourite seashells?" I burst into laughter.

Betty pressed the pause button and gave me a disappointed look. "Jill! Please! You have to take this seriously."

"Sorry, sorry. I was just—sorry. I'm ready now."

"Are you sure?"

I nodded.

"Thank you for that, Betty what are—" I fell into hysterics.

It took me some time to catch my breath. Betty was staring at me, stony-faced.

And that was pretty much the pattern for the rest of the interview. Ninety minutes later, and it was a wrap.

"Was that okay?" I asked as she showed me to the door.

"It will need a lot of editing."

"Sorry about the—you know—sorry."

"Thanks, bye."

Something told me my career as co-anchor on Betty's Sea Shell Podcast was at an end.

***

I was absolutely thrilled to find Grandma at Aunt Lucy's when I arrived. Not!

"Look what the cat's dragged in," she said.

"Mother!" Aunt Lucy scolded. "If you can't manage to buy me a card or a present, you could at least be polite to my guest."

"Excuse me for breathing, I'm sure."

I had to think of ice cream. Nothing but ice cream. Lovely ice cream sundaes. Chocolate, strawberry ice cream.

"What is wrong with everyone in this family?" Grandma sighed. "The only thing anyone thinks about is ice cream." She turned back to Aunt Lucy. "So are you going to see to my bunions or not?"

"Not. I am not spending my birthday tending to your bunions."

"Selfish." Grandma grumbled. "No consideration for others. Oh, well. I might as well get off home."

"Bye then," we both shouted.

Aunt Lucy looked at me and shook her head. "That woman will drive me insane."

"Happy birthday." I handed her the card and gift.

"That's very thoughtful of you." She gave me a hug. "It's nice to know you were thinking of me."

"I take it Grandma forgot?"

"She always forgets. I'm only her daughter, after all. When she popped round, I thought for a moment maybe she'd remembered for once, but no."

"Bunions?"

"Yeah. Apparently they'd been giving her gyp in the night. She also came around to have a moan about the Suppies."

"What's the Suppies?"

"It's the annual red carpet awards ceremony for sups. Apparently she and two other level six witches have been nominated for induction into the Suppies Hall of Fame."

"That sounds very prestigious."

"It is. Most people would be thrilled."

"Not Grandma, I'm guessing?"

"You guess right. She said the Hall of Fame is for *old* sups, and she does not consider herself to be old."

"She's ancient."

"Don't let her hear you say that for goodness sake."

"So what happens? Will she refuse the nomination?"

"She's just going to ignore it. Hopefully one of the other two will actually get the place. It wouldn't go down well if she won and then turned it down. I'm going to try not to think about it."

I'd assumed Aunt Lucy and I would go out for a walk by ourselves, but she seemed keen for us to take Barry with us. Did he know about the birthday party, I wondered? If he did, then the game would probably be up.

I needn't have worried. Barry was way too excited at the prospect of going for a walk to worry about birthday parties.

I started towards the park where I usually took Barry, but Aunt Lucy grabbed my arm.

"Why don't we go this way for a change? I know another lovely park with beautiful gardens."

"Sure. Why not?"

As we walked, Aunt Lucy talked about Lester, and how his meetings with the specialist were helping to rebuild his confidence. They were both hopeful his magic powers would be fully restored within the year. Aunt Lucy also brought up the twins and their battle with Best Cakes. Everyone had to concede that Grandma's marketing campaign was starting to pay dividends. I hoped that didn't mean I'd have to wear that stupid cupcake outfit again.

"This is nice," I said, as we stopped at the gates of the park.

"I want to run." Barry pulled at the lead.

"Let him go," Aunt Lucy said. "He'll be okay."

I wished I'd shared her confidence, but I'd spent too many hours chasing after him. Still, I had to keep her out of the house long enough for the twins to get everything set up. So, why not?

"There you go boy!"

Off he shot—who knew if I'd ever see him again?

Aunt Lucy took a deep breath. "Do you smell that?"

I did. The flower beds looked amazing. The colours and smells were intoxicating.

"That's Jethro's handiwork," she said.

"The man who looks after your garden?"

"One and the same. This is his main job. He earns a little extra on the side by working for a small number of private clients."

"You were lucky to get him."

"The twins certainly think so."

I looked at her, and she must have seen the surprise in my eyes.

"Did you think I hadn't noticed how they ogle him?" She laughed. "They're so obvious. The way they fawn all over him. It's harmless though. Neither of them would do anything to jeopardise things with their fiancé. And after all, it doesn't hurt to look. Jethro is serious eye candy."

"Aunt Lucy?"

"What? I may be getting on, but I still have eyes in my head. Have you actually seen Jethro yet?"

I shook my head.

"Prepare yourself for a treat." She pointed towards the far gate. Just in front of it, a shirtless man was working on the flower beds.

"Wow!" I said, and then had to remember to close my mouth.

"Wow, indeed. Now do you understand?"

Boy, did I understand. I thought Luther Stone was hot, but this guy was sizzling.

"I'll introduce you." Aunt Lucy took my hand.

"No." I pulled away.

"Why not?"

"I—err—we'd better find Barry. He could be anywhere."

I didn't trust myself around Jethro. I was only human after all. Wait, that's not right. But you get the gist.

I eventually tracked Barry down. He was at the boating lake. On a boat.

"Barry!"

He held up a paw—presumably waving at me. Judging by the way his tail was wagging, he was enjoying his nautical excursion.

"Is that your dog?" A man short on teeth, but not on belly, shouted at me.

"Yeah. That's Barry. Why is he in a boat?"

"That's a very good question. Why is he in a boat? These are my boats, and he hasn't paid."

"He's a dog."

"So? Same fare for everyone."

"But how did he even get into the boat?"

"He jumped in it after the last punters climbed out. It had drifted off before I could grab it."

"Can you get him back?"

"Me?" He laughed. "Your dog, your problem."

"But how am I meant to get to him?"

"I have boats for hire."

"But I don't want to sail around the lake. I just want to rescue my dog."

"Same difference. Ten pounds, please."

"That's outrageous."

"That's for two boats. Five pounds each."

"You're charging me for the dog?"

"He's in a boat isn't he?"

"Yes, but—"

"He's on the lake isn't he?"

"Yes but—"

"That'll be ten pounds, please."

I glanced back at Aunt Lucy. At least I seemed to have cheered her up—she was grinning from ear to ear.

"How do I work this thing?" I shouted to the man once I was in the boat.

"See them two long wooden things? They're called oars. Grab hold of them, and move them backwards and forwards in the water."

There was no need for sarcasm.

I hadn't realised rowing a boat could be so difficult. I'd gone back and forth, this way and that—unable to control the direction. In the meantime, Barry's boat had drifted back to shore and he'd jumped out. When I gave up through exhaustion, the owner was forced to come out onto the lake himself, throw me a line, and tow my boat back to shore.

What felt like hours later, Aunt Lucy helped me out of the boat.

"That will be another fiver," All belly and no teeth said.

"What for?"

"Having to come out and rescue you."

I would have argued, but I'd already drawn a large crowd who were chatting and laughing among themselves.

Aunt Lucy couldn't stop laughing.

"I'm sorry," she said.

"It's okay. And anyway, it is your birthday. You deserve a laugh."

"I'd almost forgotten about my birthday. I'll be glad when it's over. Are you okay? You looked terrified out there for a while."

"I'm fine." I turned to Barry. "No thanks to you."

"I like boats," Barry said. "Can we come here again?"

As we walked out of the park, I glanced over to the far gate.

Aunt Lucy must have caught my gaze because she laughed. "Looking for Jethro?"

"Who? Oh, Jethro. No, I'd forgotten all about him. I was just admiring the flowerbeds."

"Of course you were, dear. Of course you were."

Chapter 17

Aunt Lucy kept giggling to herself, and then apologising, all the way back to her house. I couldn't blame her; only I could get myself into such a mess — with Barry's help that is. If nothing else, it had lifted her out of the funk she'd been in when I arrived. Now I just had to hope the twins had done their stuff. As we reached the door, there were no sounds or signs of life inside.

"Come on in, Jill. We'll have a nice cup of tea and a piece of cake. It's my birthday, so I'm going to push the boat out." She laughed.

Everyone was a comedian.

"Surprise!" A dozen voices yelled. Party poppers cracked, and silly string covered Aunt Lucy, me and Barry. I hated that stuff.

"You!" Aunt Lucy beamed. "I should have known."

"Happy birthday, Mum!" The twins rushed over to hug and kiss their mother.

She kissed them both.

"Happy birthday, Lucy." Lester came over and gave her a kiss.

The table was full of food: sandwiches, snacks and more cakes than I'd ever seen in one place.

"Champagne!" Amber held the bottle aloft, and then popped the cork.

Everyone cheered, and sang 'happy birthday' while the champagne was poured.

"To Mum," Pearl raised her glass. "Happy birthday!"

"Happy Birthday!" echoed around the room.

An hour later the party was in full swing. Music I'd never heard before, blasted out of the speakers and most people were dancing—if you could call it that.

"What's all this noise?" Grandma had made an appearance. "I was trying to get my beauty sleep."

Beauty sleep? She'd need to sleep for a million years for it to have any effect.

"It's a party, Mother," Aunt Lucy said. "For my birthday? You remember that don't you? You were there at the time."

"No one told me about a party. Typical."

"Well you're here now," Aunt Lucy sprayed silly string over Grandma. She was way braver than me. "Why don't you help yourself to a drink?"

"Well, seeing as how I'm never going to get any sleep, I might as well. Mind you, what I really fancy is an ice cream. For some reason I can't stop thinking about them."

Pearl, Amber, Lester and me all had to look away.

By midnight, everyone was beginning to flag—except Grandma, who was still rock 'n' rolling.

"How does she do it?" Amber asked.

"She must be taking something." Pearl flopped down next to us. "It isn't natural."

"You youngsters!" Grandma came dancing over to us. "You just don't have the stamina."

"I'm going to bed," Amber said.

"Me too." Pearl started to follow her.

"Looks like you need to." Grandma cackled. "Oh, and by the way. I forgot to mention, I've rescheduled your next lesson. It's tomorrow morning at eight o'clock sharp."

***

The next morning, the three of us looked as bad as each other. My head felt like it would explode at any moment.

Barry came rushing into my room. "Walk, I want to go for a walk."

"Forget it. Aunt Lucy will take you later."

"Walk!"

"Hush. My head hurts."

He turned and walked away, sulking.

"Do you think Grandma was serious about a lesson this morning?" I said, more out of desperation than hope.

"Of course she was serious." Amber was holding a wet flannel to her forehead.

"I reckon she's doing it out of revenge." Pearl swallowed a couple of painkillers. "Did you hear what she said about the ice cream? I think she knew we'd been blocking our thoughts. That's why she's doing this."

"What would happen if we didn't show up?" I blinked my eyes to try to lessen the double vision.

"Do you really want to find out?"

I didn't. Bad as I felt, I knew the punishment for not showing up would be far worse.

***

Grandma had left word that we should meet her at the Spell-Range. We must have looked a sorry sight as we made our way there in almost total silence.

"Well, if it isn't the Terrific Three." Grandma greeted us as we stepped inside the gates.

How did she look so fresh? I'd seen her knocking back the champagne like it was going out of style, and yet here she was looking as fresh as a daisy — a very ugly daisy, but a daisy nonetheless.

"Do you remember which spell we're going to be practising today?" Grandma said.

Amber looked at Pearl. It was obvious neither of them had a clue.

"'Tie up'," I said.

"Well done. And I assume you have all been practising it as per my instructions?"

"The cake shop was extra busy this week," Amber mumbled.

"That's a no then is it?"

"Sorry Grandma."

"What about you, Pearl?"

"The tea room was extra busy too."

"Nought for two so far. Jill?"

Normally, I made a point of spending extra time on the spells which Grandma said she'd cover in the lesson. This week though I hadn't had the chance because of the kidnapping case.

"Sorry, Grandma. I've been rather tied up."

I swear I hadn't realised what I was saying until the words were already out of my mouth. Amber and Pearl looked at me as though I'd lost my mind. I had a horrible feeling I was about to lose much more than that.

"A comedian, eh?" Grandma fixed me with her evil eye.

"No, I—err—I didn't—"

"Well, seeing as how none of you have bothered to put in any practise, I'll demonstrate the spell for you."

I saw Amber and Pearl sigh with relief, but I had a bad feeling about this.

Grandma closed her eyes, raised her hand and the next thing I knew all three of us were lying on the ground—

bound from head to toe with rope.

"Grandma!" Pearl shouted. "Untie us. We're sorry."

"Sorry, what did you say?" Grandma put a hand to her ear. "I'm going a little deaf."

"Please," Amber shouted, as Grandma began to walk away.

"I have a date," I called after her.

It took us ages to get untied. We called for help, but no one was prepared to come to our assistance for fear of what Grandma might do to them. Only by rolling next to one another and pulling at the knots with our teeth, did we eventually free ourselves.

"I have to run," I shouted, already headed for the gates.

I'd arranged to meet Drake in a coffee shop close to the park where we first met. I had planned to go home after the lesson to get tidied up and changed.

***

"You really shouldn't have made such an effort." He laughed when I walked through the door. I pulled a leaf from my hair, and brushed dry mud from my jeans.

"Sorry. I had to come straight from the Spell-Range. Blame Grandma."

"Have you been upsetting her again? I thought you knew better than to do that."

Drake had finished his first drink, so he ordered a top-up and I had a flat white with two shots. I was still struggling to get going after the celebrations of the night before.

"I'm sorry I'm such a wreck," I said. "It was Aunt

Lucy's birthday yesterday, and the champagne was flowing a little too freely."

He smiled. "It's good to see you again. I wasn't sure if I ever would."

"I'm sorry about that. I behaved badly."

"It's okay."

"No, it isn't okay. I should at least have listened to your side of the story."

"My main concern right now is Raven. He's fallen in with a bad lot, and I'm worried what it might lead to. He's not a bad kid. He's just misguided."

"He must think a lot of you to come looking for me, and put me straight about your imprisonment."

"I had no idea he'd done that. Like I said before, I don't even know where he is, but at least now I know he's alive."

"I'll be happy to help you to find him. But only if you want me to."

"I'm desperate to find him, and I'm sure you could help. I don't want to put you in danger though."

"I'm a big girl. I can look after myself." I caught a glimpse of my reflection in the window. "Except when it comes to Grandma, obviously."

We laughed.

Just then my phone rang. It was Daze.

"Sorry, I have to take this."

Drake nodded.

"Where? When? Right now? I'm not really—okay, I'll be there." I ended the call, and turned back to Drake. "I'm really sorry, but something urgent has come up."

"That's okay. We'll catch up later."

***

I cast a spell, and focussed on the Washbridge address which Daze had given to me. I wasn't on my 'A' game so landed unceremoniously in a hedge next to the bench where Daze was sitting.

"Nice landing." She laughed. "What on earth happened to you?"

"It's a long story which involves Grandma and a length of rope. I'll tell you some other time."

Daze gave me the lowdown on the Rogue she was out to retrieve. Her target today was a little old lady who ran a sweet shop on the outskirts of Washbridge. I left Daze on the bench while I wandered casually across the road and peered in through the window. It was one of those shops which sold sweets from jars. It had a feel of the fifties and sixties—an era I had an affinity with. I was tempted by the sherbet dip, but that would have been unprofessional.

"Are you sure about this?" I said when I got back to Daze. "She looks like a lovely old lady."

"Of course she does. That's the whole point. If she looked like your grandmother, do you think any kids would go into her shop?"

Good point.

"So what's the plan?"

"Did you see the notice next to the door? It says *'free sweets today for kids under five'*. That's how she gets them inside."

I hadn't seen it. I'd been distracted by the sherbet dip. "What about their parents?"

"If a kid goes in with his parents, he gets the free

sweets. It's the kids that go in by themselves who are in trouble."

"Surely no kids under five would be out by themselves?"

"You'd be surprised. And besides, do you think kids who are six, seven, eight or even older wouldn't try it on? Of course they would. She prefers them young, but she'll take them any age below teens."

This sounded like the stuff of nightmares. I was still finding it hard to believe it of the sweet little old lady I'd seen behind the counter. Maybe Daze had been given bad info.

"Look!" Daze pointed to a small boy looking at the notice in the window. "He's going in."

I didn't need telling twice. I cast the 'invisible' spell followed by the 'faster' spell. I managed to reach the door just in time to sneak in after him.

"It says free sweets," the little boy said.

"So it does, sweetheart," the old lady said. "Would you like some?"

He nodded.

"Of course you would. Come with me. The free sweets are all in the back."

"Can't I have some of these?" He pointed to the liquorice torpedoes.

"Not those. The free sweets are much nicer than those. Come with me, let me show you."

As soon as he'd taken her hand, she dragged him into the back of the shop. I followed, and noticed her face had transformed from sweet old lady to wicked witch with acne. The witch hit a red button on the wall, and a huge door opened in front of her. The heat from the oven hit me in the face.

"Let me go!" the little boy screamed as she dragged him towards the oven. "I want my Mummy!"

I slammed the oven door closed, grabbed the boy's other arm and then pushed the witch to the ground.

"I'll kill you!" she screamed as she got back to her feet. "Your invisibility won't save you." She cast a spell, which must have somehow reversed my invisibility because the boy was staring at me in disbelief.

"There's plenty of room in the oven for you too!" She threw herself at me. I turned my back to her, sheltering the boy as best I could. I braced myself for the impact, but it never came.

"Let me out!" she screamed.

I turned to see the witch struggling to get free of Daze's net, but it was too late. She disappeared in a cloud of smoke.

The boy was inconsolable. He'd never get over this unless —

"There you go." I gave him a bag full of liquorice torpedoes. The 'forget' spell had wiped the horrifying ordeal from his memory.

"Thanks for your help, Jill," Daze said.

"No problem. I'm sorry I doubted you. She just looked so sweet."

"The worst ones always do."

Chapter 18

Although no body had been found, it was pretty obvious that, since finding the bloodied tee-shirt, the police now considered the Amanda Banks case to be a murder enquiry. I might not always be the best judge of character, but I didn't buy the idea that Steve Lister had murdered his girlfriend.

My next stop was the university. Steve had given me the name of one particular student, Kelly Lowe, who Amanda was friendly with. I caught up with her at lunch time.

"How was Amanda the last time you saw her?"

"Okay, I guess."

"You don't sound very sure."

"I don't want to get anyone in trouble."

"Look, Kelly. Right now we have no idea where Amanda is. She could be in danger. Every minute we waste makes it more likely this won't end well. Who are you protecting?"

"Amanda was usually bubbly, you know. I mean she was happy all the time, and she really loved Steve."

I sensed a 'but' coming.

"But that last day, she walked out of class without saying a word to the tutor. I found her in the loo. She'd been crying. When I asked her what was wrong, she said Steve was cheating on her with her best friend."

"Did she tell you her best friend's name?"

"Rachel. I don't know her last name."

"Did she say how she found out?"

"She was pretty upset. She could barely talk for crying. I think she saw them out together somewhere."

"Could she have been mistaken?"

"That's what I said. I know Steve, and he isn't the kind of guy who would cheat on her. At least, I didn't think so."

"So what happened afterwards?"

"Nothing. I wanted to go back to her flat with her, but she said she wanted to be alone." Kelly began to cry. "I shouldn't have let her go by herself. If I'd been with her maybe none of this would have happened."

"You shouldn't blame yourself. It's not your fault."

It appeared my earlier concerns about Steve and Rachel may have been on the mark. But what did that mean? Had Amanda called Steve to the holiday home to confront him? Had he lashed out and killed her, and then tried to hide it by staging the kidnapping? It simply didn't ring true. Why would she bother going to the holiday home? Why not confront him on campus or at her flat? I needed to talk to Rachel again, but when I called I got her voicemail. Her recorded message said she was out of town until the following day.

***

I ate lunch on the run as I made my way back to the office. Gordon Armitage was standing outside the building, shouting instructions to two men who were working on the sign.

"Problem with the sign, Gordon?" I said, barely hiding my grin.

He glared at me, but said nothing.

The outer office was full of people, all seated, all

knitting. Mrs V was at her desk, and she waved when she spotted me. I threaded my way through the seats.

"Did I mention the classes I'm running?" Mrs V said.

"I'm pretty sure you didn't."

"Silly me. I'd forget my head if it was loose."

"Who are all of these people?" I said in a whisper.

"They're the new people who have moved in. The 'I Am Poo' staff."

That explained where all the chairs had come from at least.

"A couple of them recognised me from Wool TV, and asked if I'd be prepared to run classes one lunch time each week."

I glanced around the room. There were women of all ages, and over by the window a solitary man.

"That's Leroy. He's a genius with the knit and purl," Mrs V said. "I've told him he should aim for the regionals."

Leroy looked up, smiled and waved a knitting needle. I smiled, and waved back.

"I'm sorry I forgot to tell you," Mrs V said. "I hope you don't mind me doing this."

"Err—no—it's fine, I guess. It might be a good idea to leave a pathway through to my office though. On the off-chance a paying client should turn up."

"Have you seen that sorry looking crowd out there?" Winky said when I made it through to my office. "They make this place look unprofessional."

"Hmm, I see you're playing darts again," I said.

Winky hit three double tops in quick succession.

"Just keeping my hand in. There's a tournament next

month."

"Where?"

"West Moreland."

"That's forty miles away."

"So?"

"How will you get there?"

"You'll take me, of course."

"No chance."

"Oh, I see. You don't mind supporting the old bag lady when she takes part in some stupid knitting competition, but you won't support me in one of the most prestigious darts tournaments of the year."

"How can you play in a tournament anyway? You're a cat."

"It's a tournament for cats. What did you think it was?"

"I—err—when is it exactly?"

**

I had no idea how I was meant to play this. My mother had asked me to pay a visit to Holly Jones, a human who'd recently lost her mother. Holly's mother and my mother were now ghost friends. Holly's mother, Maureen, had been trying to make contact with her daughter, but Holly wasn't a believer, and blocked all her attempts. I was supposed to persuade Holly that ghosts did exist, and to open herself up to contact from her mother.

Holly lived in the leafier part of Washbridge. No chewing gum or dog poo on the pavements in this part of town. The house was much as I'd expected it to be: bay windows, rose beds and a dreamcatcher.

I rang the doorbell which played something which sounded remarkably like the Wedding March.

A young woman came to the door, took one look at me (down her nose), and said, "Sorry, I don't buy anything at the door."

"Wait!"

Too late. She'd already slammed it in my face. I glanced down at the 'Welcome' mat. Oh, the irony.

I rang the doorbell again.

"My neighbour is a policeman," she said this time.

"I'm not selling anything."

"Are you sure?"

"I promise. I'm here about your mother. Your late mother."

Her demeanour changed from hostile to curious.

"My mother is—" I hesitated. "I mean *was* a friend of your mother's."

"Oh, right. Sorry about slamming the door."

"That's okay. I don't like door to door salesmen either."

"Come in. I was about to make a cup of tea. Would you like one?"

"Please."

"Milk? Sugar?"

"Milk, and one and two-thirds spoonfuls of sugar please."

I ignored the look.

"What was your mother's name?" Holly asked, once we were seated with our tea. Mine wasn't really sweet enough, but I didn't like to say anything.

"Darlene Millbright."

"It doesn't ring any bells."

"They only became acquainted recently, I believe."

"I see."

"Very recently. As in during the last few weeks."

She looked puzzled. "I think you must have got that wrong. My mother died three months ago."

"Can I ask you a question?" I said. "It may sound a little — err — strange."

"Okay."

"Do you believe in ghosts?"

"Ghosts?" She scoffed. "No of course not. What's this about?"

"I know this is going to sound kind of weird, but my mother died some time ago too. Your mother and mine became friends after they died. As ghosts."

Holly put down her cup. "I'm going to have to ask you to leave now."

"Look, I know how this sounds. I didn't believe in ghosts either when my mother first made contact."

"Please leave or I shall be forced to call the police."

She began to shepherd me to the door.

"If you just open your mind to the idea —"

The door was slammed in my face for a second time.

That went well.

I took out my card, and slid it through the letterbox. "Call me if you change your mind."

***

When I arrived back at the office, the new sign was back in working order. Not for long though. I quickly employed the 'lightning bolt' spell to knock out most of the letters again. Satisfied with my work, I started up the stairs only to encounter Gordon Armitage.

"Hi, Gordon. How's it swinging?"

"I get that you think you're funny, Jill, but I have to tell you, you're not."

"You're right. Not as funny as your sign anyway."

"That was just an unfortunate accident. It's been sorted now."

"Are you sure about that? It was still getting a few laughs when I came in just now."

"What?" He rushed down the stairs. I followed him.

A number of people were pointing and laughing at the sign which now read 'Rat Poo'.

"Switch it off!" Armitage shouted into his phone. "Turn the damn thing off!"

***

Okay, I admit it. I was now using my magical powers for purely selfish reasons. But why shouldn't I benefit? I'd put in the hours of practise after all. Even so, I still felt a little guilty when I used the 'quick snack' spell. From what I could make out it was only meant to be used in an emergency to provide a snack when you might otherwise starve.

Well—I'd kind of taken a few liberties. By the time I got home from the office, I was often shattered and the last thing I felt like doing was cooking a meal for one. So, what was I to do? If I didn't cook, and I didn't eat, then I'd probably starve. Right? Dead right. That's how I justified it to myself. It was a complicated spell, and very restrictive in what it would and wouldn't produce. The first time I tried it, I'd focussed on cheese on toast. No problem—the snack appeared right in front of me, and very tasty it was too. The next time, I tried for steak and all the trimmings, but nothing happened. Through trial and error, I'd come to realise the spell would have been better named 'fast food' because it would typically produce only the type of meal you'd find at such establishments. Not that I was complaining—it beat cooking any day, and was a heck of a lot cheaper.

I took a bite of the burger.

"Please tell me you didn't use the 'quick snack' spell again." My mother tutted.

"Mum?" I tried to say through a mouthful of burger.

"You can't live on the type of food that spell will produce."

I wiped ketchup from my mouth. "It's just a one-off."

"From what I've seen it's a one-off which happens most days. You really must eat a healthier diet otherwise you'll end up looking like Grandma."

If ever a threat was guaranteed to have maximum impact, that was it. I put the burger back on the plate. It would be salads for me from now on.

"How did you get on with Holly?" she asked.

"Not great."

"Not great as in—?"

"As in, she threw me out and threatened to call the police if I ever went back there."

"Definitely not great then. That's a pity because her mother has been clinging on to the hope that you'd be able to talk Holly round. I'm not sure how she'll take it when I tell her the news."

"Don't tell her just yet. Let me have another go. I have a few ideas up my sleeve."

"Okay. Do your best." She glanced at the burger. "And

throw that thing in the bin."

I waited until I was sure she'd gone, and then took another bite.

"Do it now!" Her voice came from out of nowhere.

Chapter 19

I had to pull the car over to the side of the road. If I hadn't, I would probably have crashed because I was laughing hysterically. Tears were streaming down my face, and it took me several minutes to compose myself enough to speak.

"Looking good!" I shouted.

The giant knitting needle turned around to face me.

"If you laugh, I'll kill you," Kathy said. Her face was the colour of beetroot.

"As if I would." I burst out laughing.

"Great! Thanks for that."

"I'm sorry." I wiped my eyes. "Don't get the needle with me." I collapsed again.

"I take back all the good things I said about your grandmother," Kathy said. "She's horrible. I'm meant to be heading up the new One-Size Needles division, not standing out here looking like a complete idiot."

"It doesn't look like there's much room for your legs in there. Careful you don't get pins and needles."

"Funny. Really funny."

"Don't split your sides laughing, or we'll have to stitch you up with needle and thread."

"Get lost, Jill."

"I'm sorry. No more needle jokes, I promise."

"You mean it?"

"Cross my heart."

"Your grandmother has launched a web site: EverAWoolMoment.com. It offers one hour delivery anywhere in the country. She decided the launch needed a push, and after the success of the Everlasting Wool campaign, she decided this was the way to go. Do you want to know the ironic thing?"

"Go on."

"I was the one who told her I thought it was a great idea. Little did I know that she intended me to wear this stupid thing."

"One hour delivery? Anywhere in the country? How can she do that?"

"Beats me. I have no idea where the stock is being held or who is doing the delivery. It's all very hush, hush."

"How long do you have to stay out here?"

"Only this morning, thank goodness. Anyway, how are you?"

"I'm fine."

"What about the kidnap case?"

"Ongoing. How are the kids?"

"Great. Mikey's not very happy though because he can't find the last card he needs to complete his collection of football stickers. He's tried everywhere, poor lamb."

"Bit like trying to find a needle in a haystack then?" I dissolved into hysterics yet again.

Grandma's wool empire was expanding, and as far as I could tell, it owed most of its success to magic. How was she getting away with it?

***

I met Rachel Nixon at her flat.

"How's Steve?" She looked concerned. "Have you seen him?"

"Yes, but only briefly. He appears to be holding it together."

"Why did they arrest him? I don't understand."

"Were you and Steve seeing one another?"

"What do you mean 'seeing' one another?"

"Like an item."

"Me and Steve? No! Are you crazy? Why would you even think that?"

"He was here the last time I came."

"We're friends. We were both upset about Amanda. No, of course we aren't an item."

"Amanda thought you were."

Rachel flopped down into a chair. She looked completely stunned. "No. Why would she think that? Who told you that?"

"She told someone at uni on the same day as she disappeared. Apparently she saw you and Steve together."

"That doesn't make any sense. Why would she think there was anything between Steve and me?"

"Apparently Steve told her he was staying in, but then she saw him with you."

"Where? Oh, wait. I know. We were planning a surprise birthday party for her."

"Just you and Steve?"

"No. Tom was supposed to be there too, but he never showed up."

"Who's Tom?"

"The bar manager where Amanda worked—works. It was his idea. He said we should meet up to make plans, but then he never showed up. That's why Steve told Amanda he was staying in. But how did she see us? She was never there—was she?"

If Rachel was lying, she was one of the best liars I'd ever

met. To corroborate her story, I was going to have to speak to Tom. I called the bar. The person who answered sounded half-asleep, but managed to inform me that Tom wouldn't be in until that evening.

***

Mrs V wasn't at her desk, but she'd left me a note. It was rather cryptic, and looked as though it had been dashed off in a hurry. It simply said: *'Gone to meet man at Wool TV'*.

"Winky, what's going on with Mrs V?"

He meowed and scratched his ear.

"Did you hear her take a phone call?"

More meowing.

"I'm not falling for that one again. What kind of mug do you think I am?"

He meowed.

"And why is this window wide open?" I turned around just in time to see Winky launch himself at me—teeth bared, and claws out.

"What are you doing?" I yelled just before he hit me full on in the chest. He was clawing at my body while doing his best to sink his teeth into my throat. The sheer force with which he'd hit me had sent me staggering backwards, so I was now leaning back against the open window.

He was strong. Much too strong for a cat—even a psycho cat. I cast the 'power' spell, spun around and tore him from my body, sending him flying out of the open window.

I couldn't bear to look down at the street below. I

staggered backwards until I came to rest — leaning against the desk. Only when my breathing began to slow down did I hear the noise.

A scratching sound was coming from the bottom drawer of the filing cabinet, so I slid it open slowly.

"Winky!"

He mumbled something which I couldn't quite make out because of the tape over his mouth. His legs were bound too.

I lifted him onto the desk, grabbed the scissors and cut the binding on his legs.

"This is going to hurt." I grabbed the tape, and pulled it off.

"Ouch! Ouch! That hurt!"

"Sorry. What happened?"

"What do you think happened? Someone tied me up and stuck me in the filing cabinet."

"Who?"

"How would I know? I was fast asleep and the next thing I know — bang — I'm in the filing cabinet. I bet it was the old bag lady — she hates me."

"Mrs V would never do anything like that. And besides, there was another cat in here when I walked in. He tried to kill me."

"What did he look like?"

"Like you. I thought it *was* you until he went for my throat."

"Where is he now?"

"I threw him out of the window."

"Nice one." He jumped down off the desk and up onto the window sill.

"He isn't there now."

Winky was right. There was no sign of the impostor, but then I suspected that whatever it was that had attacked me hadn't actually been a cat. Every instinct told me this was the work of The Dark One.

***

I'd died and gone to heaven. Or at least that's how good it felt when I spotted it. I'd needed something to calm my nerves after the cat attack, so I'd headed to the local coffee shop. They had introduced a new line of biscuits. When I say new, they weren't exactly new—they were old favourites. There was a jaffa cake, a jammy dodger and several others including the king of biscuits, and my personal favourite, the custard cream. What was so good about these was that they were GIANT biscuits. They were at least four times the size of their standard counterparts. A giant custard cream! And as if it couldn't get any better, each of the giant custard creams was wrapped in cellophane, so there was no contamination from other, inferior biscuits.

"A skinny latte and two giant custard creams, please."

"Two?" The young woman behind the counter looked rather shocked.

"Sorry. Did I say two? I meant one." Slip of the tongue obviously. No one would be that greedy.

***

Bar Bravo was a small bar located in a street full of similar bars—all pretty much interchangeable. I deliberately arrived shortly after opening time when I hoped it would still be quiet.

Quiet wasn't the word for it—dead would have been more accurate. There were maybe six or seven customers, and behind the bar: a young woman with multicoloured hair, and a man with a shaven head, and tattoos on his upper arms.

"I'm looking for Tom."

"The man chewed his gum while appraising me. Judging by the other people in the bar, I didn't fit their normal demographic.

"I'm Tom," he replied, eventually.

I gave him my card and explained I was working on the kidnap case.

"Amanda was a sweet kid," he said.

"Was?"

"Not looking good for her after all this time is it?"

"There's no reason to believe she's dead." Even as I said it, I wasn't totally convinced. "Rachel Nixon gave me your name."

"Sure, I know Rachel. She comes in here occasionally. Sometimes her and Amanda go on to a club after Amanda finishes her shift."

"One of Amanda's friends from uni told me she was upset on the day she disappeared. How did she seem to you the night before?"

"She was okay. I remember her being quite bubbly actually."

"Are you sure?"

"Positive. I'd have noticed if there had been anything wrong."

"What can you tell me about the birthday party?"

"Oh, you mean the surprise party for Amanda?"

"Yeah. Rachel Nixon said you'd arranged to meet her and Steve to plan everything, but then you didn't show."

"That's right. A couple of the staff phoned in sick, so I couldn't get away."

The bar was beginning to fill up now. Another young woman had joined Tom and the girl with multi-coloured hair behind the bar. I gave Tom my card, and asked him to give me a call if he thought of anything which might help.

I was only a few metres down the road when I heard someone call after me. It was the girl from the bar—the one with multi-coloured hair.

"I overheard you talking about Amanda." As she spoke, she looked back over her shoulder as though checking no one had followed her. "I'm Carrie. I work with Amanda. She's really nice."

"Do you know something that might help?"

She glanced back at the bar again, obviously nervous.

"What Tom told you back there. It wasn't true. Amanda was really upset that night; the day before the kidnapping. I found her crying."

"Do you know why she was upset?"

"She didn't have time to tell me before Tom came and dragged me back to the bar. When I went to check on her later, she'd left. She didn't finish her shift."

"Do you have any idea why she might have been so upset?"

"The only thing I know is that Tom and Amanda left the bar for a short while. They never said where they were going. Amanda was okay when she left, but then a total mess when she came back."

"Do you think he did something to her?"

"I don't know. I suppose he might have tried it on with her, but she would have told him to do one. She was crazy in love with Steve."

"I don't suppose you know any of Tom's ex girlfriends do you?"

"I could probably find you some phone numbers. He's always leaving his phone under the bar."

"That would be great. Here." I passed her my card. "Give me a call if you manage it."

Chapter 20

My powers of persuasion, however good they might be, were never going to work on Holly Jones. If I turned up at her door again, she'd slam it in my face. And this time, she'd probably call the police. To her, I was the mad woman who believed our mothers had become acquainted since they died. I was the loony who saw ghosts. Persuasion was out, so I had to come up with another approach.

I waited until it was dark and then sneaked around the back of her house. There was a large bush close to the patio doors, and from behind there, I could see Holly seated on the sofa. She appeared to be engrossed in something on TV. I had my fingers crossed that this would work. I'd been practising the 'move' spell which was actually above my grade—it was level four. It was one of the spells Grandma had used to see how far she could push me—something she did every now and then. I'd never tried to use it through glass before, but I was hopeful it would work. Even if it did, I was much further away from the objects than I'd been when I practised this spell before. Oh well. Here goes nothing.

On my previous visit, I'd seen a photograph on the bookcase behind the sofa. I was fairly sure it was a photo of Holly's mother. The woman was certainly in the right age range. I took a deep breath, cast the spell, and focused on the photo frame. It started to rise, so at least I knew I could use the spell through glass. If I lost control of the object it would drop to the floor, and most likely break. Slowly, I began to move the photo through the air until it was over the drinks cabinet, which was close to the sofa.

Whatever Holly was watching, it must have been good because she didn't take her eyes off the TV screen. When I was sure the photo was over the drinks cabinet I lowered it until it was maybe a half-inch above, and then let it drop.

The noise made Holly jump. She looked around as though expecting to see someone standing behind her. She seemed to do a double-take before standing up, and walking over to the drinks cabinet. She stared at the photo, and then looked across at the bookcase. Confusion was etched on her face. After a few moments she put the photo back onto the bookcase, returned to the sofa, and continued her viewing. She must have somehow convinced herself she'd moved it.

If at first you don't succeed — bring out the big guns. Invisibility baby!

I cast the spell, checked my reflection in the window to make sure it had worked, and then rang the doorbell. I wondered if my mother was watching me. She was probably busy smooching with Alberto somewhere.

"Yes, I am watching you." The voice came from behind me, and almost made me jump out of my skin. But, before I could turn around, the door opened and Holly appeared.

We were face to face and only inches apart, but she couldn't see me.

"Hello?" She had the same confused look on her face as the locksmith had the first time I ever used this spell. "Anyone there?"

She took a few steps forward out onto the driveway. I skirted around her and into the house. Let the fun begin.

Holly mumbled something about kids being a pain in the backside, then closed the door and came back into the living room. I was standing directly behind the sofa where she resumed her TV viewing. She was watching some awful reality TV show—why did people watch that rubbish? I leaned forward and pressed the channel change button. The TV switched to a wildlife programme—much better. Holly obviously didn't agree. She muttered something, and switched back to the reality show. Undeterred I changed channel again. She picked up the remote, gave it a good shake and changed back again. This wasn't working, so I picked up the remote, and walked over to the TV. Holly's eyes were wide, and her mouth was open, as she watched the remote control seemingly float across the room. That seemed to get her attention. She pulled her knees up to her chest, and looked around the room.

"Who's there? If this is meant to be a joke, it isn't funny! Come out or I'll call the police."

She didn't look as though she was about to call the police—she looked too scared to move. I should have felt bad—yeah well—I was having too much fun. I walked over to the window, and closed the blinds, and then opened them again.

Holly picked up her phone. Oh no! She *was* going to call the police. I had to get out of there. But before I could, she jumped off the sofa, ran to the door and stepped outside. What was I supposed to do now? Time was running out. Any second now, the invisibility would wear off. I was trapped in her house, and couldn't leave through the door because she was right outside.

Just then my phone rang. Bum! I managed to grab it on the first ring—hopefully Holly hadn't heard it.

"Hello?" I said in a whisper.

"Is that Jill?"

I heard those words in stereo: On my phone and through the door. It was Holly.

"Jill, speaking."

"I can barely hear you. Can you speak up?"

I was visible now. If she came back into the house, the game would be up. I had to keep her talking while I gave myself time to think. I made my way upstairs, and into the first bedroom I came to.

"Is that better?" I said in my normal voice.

"Yes, I can hear you now. You said I could ring you if—err—if I—err"

"Have you seen your mother's ghost?"

"No, yes. I don't know. Some strange things have been happening."

"What kind of strange things?"

"The TV switched channel. Then the remote floated across the room. And the window blinds opened and closed."

"That's probably your mother trying to get in touch with you."

"But there are no such things as ghosts."

"Then why did you call me?"

"I—err—I don't understand what's happening."

"Look. I know you are finding this hard, but why not open your mind to the possibility? What harm can it do? If you're right, and there are no such things as ghosts then you've lost nothing. But if you're wrong, you get to see your mother again. Isn't it worth a try?"

"I'm not sure."

"Okay. Well give me another call if you change your mind."

"No! Wait! What would I have to do?"

"If you're ready to give it a try, I'll come around there and talk you through it."

"When could you come?"

"Right away. I'm quite close by."

"Okay. I'll give it a try."

"That's good. You won't regret it."

I heard the door handle. Oh no! I had to stop her.

"Holly! Is there a florist near to you?"

"A florist?" I heard her release the door handle. She was still outside. Phew!

"It will help to smooth your mother's transition if you welcome her with flowers." Boy, I was pulling this stuff out of my backside.

"There isn't a florist for miles, and besides they'll be closed by now. The supermarket sells flowers though. That's only a couple of streets away."

"Ideal. Go around there now. Buy your mum's favourite flowers. By the time you get back, I'll be waiting at your door."

"Okay. I'll see you shortly."

I watched her through the window. Once she was out of sight, I hurried downstairs, and out of the door. That was close.

Holly arrived back fifteen minutes later with a bunch of roses in her hand.

"Hi," I greeted her.

"This is all they had, I'm afraid." She held out a sorry looking bunch of flowers.

"Did your mum like roses?"

"She preferred tulips, but they didn't have any."

"I'm sure they'll be fine. Shall we go in?"

Holly looked nervous, so I led the way. "It's okay, come through."

She followed me into the living room, her eyes darting back and forth.

"Is she here now?" she said, her voice wavering.

"She won't be far away."

"So what happens now?"

"You need to do two things. Call her name, and remove all trace of doubt or scepticism from your mind. Can you do that?"

"I'll try."

She looked at me for reassurance. I smiled, and nodded for her to start.

"Maureen, Maureen!"

"Hold on. Did you call your mother Maureen when she was alive?"

"No. I called her Mum."

"Then that's what you should call her now."

"Mum, Mum."

"Clear your mind of all doubt. You have to believe she is going to be with you again. Try again."

She closed her eyes. "Mum, Mum. Please show yourself to me."

She opened her eyes, and the expression on her face told me my work was done. I couldn't see her mum's ghost because she was attached to Holly, but I knew she'd appeared. Holly was beaming, and was already in conversation with her.

She didn't even see me sneak out of the house.

"Well done, Jill." My mother appeared next to me on the driveway. "Thanks very much for that."

"My absolute pleasure."

Jill Gooder — P.I. and ghost whisperer.

The next morning, Armitage's sign was still switched off. Score one for the Gooder. Mrs V was in a good mood, and was obviously bursting to tell me something.

"Aren't you going to ask why I'm so happy?"

"Nah."

Her face dropped.

"Only kidding. Of course I want to know."

"I've been offered a part-time role as a roving reporter for Wool TV. Don't worry it won't interfere much with my work here."

What a relief. I wouldn't have wanted the production of scarves and socks to suffer.

"What will you be doing exactly?"

"I'll be interviewing the movers and shakers in the yarn industry."

"Are there any? It seems such a sedate type of business."

"Don't kid yourself. Yarn is a cut-throat business. Dog eat dog."

Who knew?

"My first interview will be with your grandmother. She has caused quite a stir in the industry with her Everlasting Wool and One-Size Needles."

I bet she has, and there'd be even more of a stir if people knew the truth. "Make sure you grill her."

"Don't worry, I will. Woodstein and Bernwood have nothing on me."

As I was talking with Mrs V, I heard voices on the landing outside the office. I cracked the door open just wide enough to get a glimpse of Gordon Armitage talking to a man dressed in overalls. Armitage must have spotted me because he halted mid-sentence, and led the man away down the stairs. Perhaps it was the latest attempt to repair the sign. Or maybe something more sinister. I was under no illusion that Armitage still wanted me out, and I wouldn't have put it past him to be planning something underhanded.

I gave it a few minutes, and then sneaked down the stairs. By the time I got outside, Armitage had disappeared. The other man was climbing into a cradle which was suspended from the top of our building. The cradle began to ascend, and I realised that he wasn't there to repair the sign. He had a bucket of water, and was apparently cleaning the windows. Except that he wasn't. Although the sign on the side of the cradle read 'Windows Bright', the man was doing no more than wave a chamois leather around. I was sure he was up to something, and he was headed to the window of my office. That's when I spotted it. He had a camera.

I made it up the stairs in record time, burst through the door, past a startled Mrs V, and into my office. The man's head was just poking up above the bottom of the window. Winky was watching from his usual windowsill spot. If the man got a photo of Winky, Gordon Armitage would take it to the landlord. The terms of my lease didn't allow animals in the office, so I had to do something, and I had to do it right now.

I cast the 'illusion' spell just as the man's head appeared

above the window ledge. He took one glance at Winky, and then stepped back in horror. He only just managed to grab a hold of the cradle and stop himself falling to the floor. He still looked terrified as he pressed the lever to send it back down. Once it was on the ground, he jumped out and ran away as fast as his legs would carry him.

"What was wrong with him?" Winky looked confused.

"Your ugly face scared him off."

"Well that's charming. I love you too."

What had actually happened was that the poor man had looked at Winky, and seen a lion growling at him.

Up yours, Armitage!

Chapter 21

Where was the stupid thing? I had it with me when I came home last night, but what had I done with it? Don't you hate it when you lose your phone? What? You never lose it? Well aren't you the organised one then?

It was in the flat somewhere. If I'd had a landline, I could have called it and listened for the ring, but who had landline phones at home these days? Then, as if to prove I could be even stupider than I thought was possible, I came up with a brain wave. I could ask Kathy to call me.

Just one slight problem with that plan—I didn't have a phone to call Kathy to ask her to call me. Oh bum! I needed a custard cream. Or maybe two. No more than three—that would be greedy. I popped open the Tupperware box, and lo and behold—

"There you are!"

My phone was snuggled up among the custard creams.

I had a missed call from a number I didn't recognise. There was no voice message, so I called the number.

"Hello?" a female voice answered.

"You called my number. This is Jill Gooder."

"Oh, hi. It's Carrie from Bar Bravo."

"Hi."

"I said I'd call you if I managed to get the numbers off Tom's phone. I've managed to get three if that helps?"

"That's great."

She sent me a text with the phone numbers of three women Tom had dated. I called each of them in turn.

Fortunately for me, none of them was reluctant to talk.

Just the opposite in fact. They didn't have a good word to say about Tom between them. One of them, Caroline, obviously thought I was dating him, and warned me in no uncertain terms to get away from him. All three of them told very similar tales. Caroline had worked at Bar Bravo for a few months. Tom had been charming at first—quite the gentleman.

"He has the gift of the gab," she said. "He could charm the birds out of the trees—that's what my mum used to say. But he's a pathological liar. And a control freak. While I was doing what he wanted, everything was okay, but if I didn't—"

She hesitated, and for a moment I thought I'd lost the call.

"Caroline?"

"Sorry. I haven't told anyone else about this."

"It's okay. Take your time."

"He hit me."

The tears began to flow.

"He hit me because I hadn't told him I was going out with a friend. It was a girl friend, mind you. We only went for a quick drink after college. He went crazy. I thought—"

She hesitated again.

"I thought he was going to kill me."

"Did you report it to the police?"

"No. I know I should have done, but I just wanted to put it behind me. I quit the job at Bar Bravo, and moved to another flat. He kept on calling me for a long time after I'd moved, but I never answered. I would have changed my number, but so many other people have it."

I thanked her for her time.

The other two women, Debbie and Paula, told remarkably similar stories. Tom had been the perfect gentleman — charming and funny. Right up until the point where he became aggressive, controlling and violent. Both of them had been struck by him on at least one occasion. Neither of them had reported the assault.

It wasn't difficult to conclude that Tom was bad news, and I couldn't help but wonder if Amanda's disappearance was connected to her being upset the previous night when she'd come back to the bar with him. He had now become my primary focus.

I made another call to Carrie. She was able to give me Tom's home address, and to confirm that Friday was his day off.

***

It was my own fault. I'd become quite adept at avoiding Mr Ivers, but I'd completely forgotten about his makeover, and so I almost walked straight into him.

"Morning, Jill."

"Oh — err — morning. I nearly didn't recognise you."

"Your cousins did a great job."

I had to hand it to the twins; the transformation was remarkable.

"How is the newspaper column going?"

"Good." He smiled. "Mostly."

"Is there a problem?"

"Not with the column exactly. That practically writes itself. It's just that — "

I was intrigued now. Who'd have thought I'd ever use the word 'intrigued' in relation to Mr Ivers?

"Well, I had hoped to pick up more fans."

"Aren't many people reading the column?"

"Oh, yeah. The Bugle is very pleased with the numbers and the feedback so far."

"So? I don't understand."

"I thought I might have attracted more female readers. That's why I got you to organise the makeover for me."

I smiled. So all along Mr Ivers' master plan was to use the movie review column to attract groupies.

"I take it that hasn't happened?"

"No. Almost all of the feedback has come from men—other movie buffs."

So, other sad sacks then. "That's rather disappointing. Maybe that will change over time."

"I hope so. I've provided the Bugle with a new photo. I have my collar open on this one."

"Nice." That should have them knocking the door down.

"I assume you've been reading my column?"

"Me—err—is that my phone? I think my landline is ringing. Sorry, got to dash."

I hurried back to the refuge of my flat.

I gave it twenty minutes until I was sure the coast was clear, and then made another attempt to leave.

"Hello, Jill."

Oh bum! "Hi, Betty. I'm on my way to the office. Running a bit late."

"I thought you'd want to hear how the first podcast went."

Not really. "Of course. How did it go?"

"Good." She smiled. "Mostly."

Deja vu.

"I've had some feedback on the content from other people who are interested in sea shells."

"Well that's good. Isn't it?"

"Yes, I'm very pleased with that."

"But?"

"Most of the feedback has been commenting on how sexy the voice on the podcast is." She shook her head.

"I shouldn't worry too much about that kind of person. They're obviously shallow minded and not worthy of your time. Why would someone comment on your voice like that?"

"No, it wasn't *my* voice they were commenting on. I had tons of feedback from men saying how sexy *your* voice was. But like you say, such people are so shallow."

"*My* voice? People thought I had a sexy voice? Men?"

"Shallow men."

"Absolutely. Shallow. I don't suppose you have their names? Email addresses? No, of course not."

"Have you heard the news?" Betty said, as I made to get away.

"What's that?"

"Someone new is moving in upstairs. Into number six. The one that's been empty ever since I moved in."

"It's been empty for almost a year. Since the incident with the cheese grater."

"Cheese grater?"

"It's a long story. Some other time, maybe. Have you actually met our neighbour-to-be?"

"No, but I hear he's a bookkeeper."

Great! I was beginning to feel like the only cool kid in a building full of losers. What? I'm cool—P.I.s are very cool.

Still, the new neighbour sounded as though he might be a perfect match for Betty.

***

It was a beautiful day. The sky was blue, and the sun was beating down. Candlefield seemed to get more than its fair share of good weather. Was that just coincidence or was magic influencing the weather system? Who knew?

"Jill!" Amber called to me when I arrived at Aunt Lucy's door. She was walking down the street, arm in arm with William. She appeared to be carrying a picnic basket.

"Hello you two. Is it your day off?"

"It shouldn't be." Amber suddenly looked rather guilty. "Officially, I'm in my bedroom with a bad tummy ache." She giggled. "Pearl is holding the fort."

"I see." This had the makings of trouble.

"William and me are going on a picnic." She held up the basket.

"So I see. Very nice. Well you certainly have the weather for it."

"Why don't you come with us?"

"Oh no. I'm not playing gooseberry."

"Please, Jill. William doesn't mind, do you?"

"Of course not." He flashed me a smile. "You should come."

Just then, a red, soft top sports car pulled up alongside us.

"I knew it!" Pearl was in the passenger seat—her gaze burning into her sister. "I knew you were faking it."

Amber blushed. "I *was* poorly, but it passed."

"Liar. What's that?"

"We're going on a picnic."

"And leaving muggins here to look after the shop? I don't think so."

"What are you doing here, anyway?" Amber said. "You can't just walk out of the shop."

"Why not? You did. And anyway, Jean and Sally can cope. Alan and I are going for a picnic too, aren't we Alan?"

"Yes, babe." He gave her a peck on the cheek.

Amber screwed up her face. "Do you have to do that in public?"

Pearl ignored her sister and turned to me.

"Jill, why don't you jump in and come with us?"

"She's already said she'd come with us!" Amber protested.

"We have much better food."

"We have wine."

"Jill, jump in."

"No, Jill. You said you'd come with us."

I raised my hand for silence. "Enough! I came here because it was a lovely day, and I thought I'd get some peace and quiet. I haven't agreed to go with either of you, and I don't intend to."

"But, Jill—"

"Please, Jill—"

"Hush. Because it's such a beautiful day, I'm going to go on a picnic. Now if any of you wish to come with *me*, then you are more than welcome. But on one condition. If you two start arguing—even once—I'll magic myself straight back to Washbridge. Is that clear?"

"But—"

"Yes, but—"

"Is that clear?"

"Yes."

"Crystal."

"Good. Well let's see if I can persuade Aunt Lucy to knock me up a picnic, and then we'll be on our way. And I expect you two—" I looked from Amber to Pearl and then back again, "to be on your best behaviour."

As I made my way into Aunt Lucy's house, I could hear the twins grumbling.

"She's so bossy."

"I know. Grandma has nothing on her."

***

Aunt Lucy came through. I had enough sandwiches, cake, fruit and soft drinks to feed a family.

"Why don't you come with us?" I said to Aunt Lucy. "Goodness knows, there's enough food."

"I'd like to, but Jethro is coming this afternoon to feed the lawn. I should be here to supervise."

Judging by the glint in her eye, I was beginning to think the twins weren't the only ones who were enthralled by Jethro. Maybe I should stay back too. After all, Jethro was super hot.

"If Lucy can't go, I can always make up the numbers."

I turned around to come nose to wart with Grandma.

"I've always enjoyed a good picnic."

"Grandma. I didn't see you there."

"So, can I come with you?"

"With us? On the picnic?"

"That's what I said."

"Right. I'll just need to check with the girls. I won't be a minute."

The twins were still looking daggers at one another when I got back outside.

"Grandma wants to know if she can come with us."

"What?" Amber's face fell.

"You're joking." Pearl shook her head. "What did you tell her?"

"I haven't yet."

"What do you think?" Amber looked crestfallen.

Pearl shrugged. "We might as well go back to work. It would be more fun."

"Excuse me." The man's voice caught me by surprise. I'd been so taken up by the discussion about Grandma that I hadn't seen him standing outside her house. "Do you know if the lady who lives here is in?"

"Who are you?"

"I'm from the Candle. I'm here to interview her about her nomination for the Suppies Hall of Fame. Do you happen to know where she might be?"

"Is she expecting you?"

"Not really. I've tried to contact her a couple of times, but no joy."

"Well, I'm sure she'll be more than happy to give you an interview," I said, ignoring the looks from the twins. "She's very excited about her nomination." I beckoned him over. "She's actually in here. This is my Aunt's house." I opened the door. "In you go."

"Don't you want to check with her first?"

"No need. She'll be pleased to see you." I gave him a nudge in the back. "In you go."

As soon as he was inside, I pushed the door shut.

"Come on, run for it."

I jumped into the back seat of Alan's car. Amber and William exchanged a glance, and then followed suit. It was a tight squeeze, but there was just enough room for the three of us.

"Go!" I yelled.

Alan hit the gas, and we flew up the hill and away.

"We are so dead," Amber looked back down the hill.

"It was Jill's idea." Pearl laughed.

"Gee, thanks. What were we meant to do? She wouldn't have expected us to hang around while she did her interview."

Would she?

Chapter 22

"Maybe we should have waited for Grandma." I took a bite out of one of the egg and cress sandwiches which Amber had brought. The twins were watching me like a hawk to see whose sandwiches I ate the most of. But I was on to them, so I made sure to eat the same number from each of them. What? Don't tell *me* it's petty—I'm not the one keeping score.

"It was your idea to leave her behind." Pearl giggled.

"Yeah, we totally wanted to wait for her." Amber giggled too.

"Thanks you two. Nice to know who your friends are."

"Don't say that, Jill. You know we're only kidding."

"So if Grandma asks whose idea it was to go without her, what will you say?"

The twins glanced at one another, and then back at me.

"We'll totally throw you under the bus," Amber said.

"Totally."

"Great."

"But we won't enjoy doing it."

"That's okay then."

The sun was still beating down; there wasn't a cloud to be seen. Alan had driven us to a small country park which was new to me. The guys, William and Alan, were tossing a Frisbee to and fro. The park was full of families, all taking advantage of the weather to enjoy a picnic.

"You should have asked Drake to come with us," Pearl said.

"I did have coffee with him the other day."

"How did it go?"

"Okay, I guess. He's worried about his brother. I said

I'd try to help find him. Ouch!"

"Sorry." Alan came running over to collect the Frisbee which had just clipped the back of my ear. "Are you okay?"

"Yeah, I'm fine."

And then the heavens opened, and rain began to pour down on us.

And I mean, only on us!

"Look!" I shouted, pointing to another family seated only fifty metres away.

"It's only raining on us." Amber was trying to cover her head with a serviette.

We all looked up to see a single dark cloud hovering directly above us.

"Run for the car!" William shouted.

We gathered up our belongings as best we could, and raced over to the car. The dark cloud followed us every step of the way.

"Put the top up!" Pearl yelled.

It seemed to take an age before the top was in place. The five of us were dripping wet from head to toe. The twins looked at me and we all said in unison, "Grandma!"

The boys dropped us off outside Cuppy C. We dripped our way upstairs, and took turns to shower. Amber went downstairs to fetch us all a coffee, and the three of us sat on Pearl's bed with our drinks.

"We have to get our own back," I said.

The girls stared at me, and then burst out laughing.

"I'm serious. We can't let her treat us like this. We have to show her she can't push us around."

"Yeah, good luck with that."

"Let us know how you get on."

"Cowards. Well I'm not going to stand for it even if you two are chicken."

"Cluck, cluck."

"Cluck."

I was wasting my time with those two. They were way too scared of Grandma to do anything, but I was determined to get my revenge.

***

Rather than go straight back to Washbridge, I decided to call in on Aunt Lucy. Maybe she'd have some ideas on how I could get even with Grandma.

Her door was unlocked, as per usual.

"Aunt Lucy?"

There was no reply.

"Aunt Lucy? It's Jill."

Still no reply.

I walked through to the living room, and spotted her in the garden. She was not alone.

"Jill. I wasn't expecting you back yet. How was the picnic, and what happened to your hair?"

"Aunt Lucy, why do you have a goat in the garden?"

"You may well ask. Jethro had no sooner finished treating the lawn than Grandma decided she'd had enough of that journalist from The Candle."

I did a double-take at the goat. "Is that him?"

Aunt Lucy nodded. "The spell should only last for another hour or so, but I'll probably have no lawn left by then." She glanced again at my hair.

"There was a heavy downpour while we were at the

park. We got soaked."

"Really? It's been lovely here."

"I suspect it's been lovely everywhere except for where we were. I think Grandma used the 'rain' spell on us because we sneaked off without her."

Aunt Lucy laughed. "That sounds like something she would do."

"I'm getting fed up with the way she treats us. There must be something we can do about it?"

"Like what?"

"I don't know. How have you all put up with it for so long?"

"You shouldn't let her get to you like this."

"I can't help it. Some days, I just want to strangle her."

"Come inside." She beckoned me to follow her. "Let's have a nice cup of tea. That will make you feel better."

It didn't. I was still livid—even after a cup of tea and a chocolate cupcake.

"Can I give you one piece of advice, Jill?"

I nodded.

"Patience."

"I don't really do patient."

"You have to try. Wait until you've progressed up the levels; until your magic is a match for Grandma's."

"That's going to take forever."

"Not at the rate you're progressing. When you are much more advanced than you are now, you'll be in a position to give as good as you get when it comes to Grandma and her magic."

"Until then?"

"Try not to upset her."

"How do I do that?"

"I don't know, but if you work it out, let me know."

We both laughed. I knew Aunt Lucy was right. I shouldn't allow Grandma to get under my skin.

But it was easier said than done.

***

The next morning I was up bright and early. Fortunately there was a small shopping area across the road from where Tom lived. I parked up, sat in my car and waited. I wasn't exactly sure what I was hoping to see, but I had a feeling the bar manager was somehow involved in the kidnapping.

Two hours later, and I was still waiting—he obviously wasn't an early riser. I was hungry and thirsty, but daren't risk going into the shops in case he made an appearance and I missed him.

It was almost midday when he finally showed up. Even from that distance, I could tell he'd only just got up. He was yawning and stretching all the way to the small silver Fiat, which was parked in front of his block of flats. I tucked in right behind him—I figured he wouldn't be expecting a tail, and was probably still too asleep to notice anyway. He headed straight for the motorway.

Sometimes my own stupidity astounded me. What was I thinking? The little orange light on the dashboard wasn't there for show—it meant I was driving on fumes! Idiot! I didn't dare drive past the next petrol station—if I did the car wouldn't make it more than another couple of miles.

I slammed the nozzle into the tank, and after what seemed like an eternity, rushed into the shop to pay.

"Good morning, Madam."

"Morning." Hurry up.

"It's a lovely day, isn't it?"

"Lovely." Quicker.

"Do you have a loyalty card?"

"No." Come on!

"Would you like one?"

"No." Give me strength.

"Enter your PIN."

I did.

"Chocolate is on two for one today."

"No thanks!"

I put my foot to the floor and gave chase. Tom must have been at least five minutes ahead of me. If he'd turned off anywhere, it was game over. Fifteen minutes later, I was about to give up when I spotted him in the distance.

"Yes!"

I tucked in behind him once again, and followed for another twenty two miles before he turned off the motorway. From there, he headed out into the countryside into an area I wasn't familiar with. There was way less traffic now, and he was much more likely to spot me.

He made a sudden right onto what was little more than a dirt track. If I followed him up there he'd soon realise I was tailing him, so instead, I parked in a lay-by close to the track, and then followed on foot. The track cut through a wooded area, so I couldn't see his car. I needed to keep my guard up in case he'd already spotted me and this was a trap.

***

The farmhouse looked as though it had been neglected for many years. Tom's car was parked next to the house, but there was no sign of him. Once I stepped out from the cover of the trees, there was an expanse of open ground. If he was at the windows—it was impossible to tell from that distance—he would inevitably see me. Unless—

I cast the 'faster' spell, and a split second later I was standing with my back to the wall of the house. Even if he'd been looking out of the window, I would have been moving too fast for him to see me. Next, I cast the 'listen' spell, and focussed on the sounds coming from inside the house. There were two voices: a man and a woman.

"When?" she said.

"Soon." I could hear the impatience in Tom's voice.

"You said we could go as soon as we had the money."

"Shut up! We'll go when I say so."

"I can't stay here another night. It's so cold, and I'm starving."

"I'm sick of hearing you whinge. Shut up or I'll shut you up!"

"No, please! I'm sorry."

That was my cue. I tried the door handle, but it was locked. I cast the 'power' spell and pushed it clean off its hinges.

The two of them turned to look at me. The way the young woman was cowering suggested she thought Tom was about to hit her.

"Step away from her!"

He took a step back, but in the same movement, grabbed a knife from the table behind him.

"I'd put that down if I was you," I said, trying to sound calmer than I felt.

"Or you'll do what exactly?"

I'd expected him to advance on me, but instead he stepped behind the chair where the young woman was sitting, and put the blade to her throat. I could see the terror in her eyes.

"Get out of here or I'll kill her!" he spat the words.

My aim had to be perfect or she would be dead.

It was the first time I'd applied such focus to the 'lightning bolt' spell. Normally, I'd point my finger and hope for the best. This time I focussed on a specific target—the hand holding the knife.

Tom screamed in pain, and dropped the blade. That was my chance. I kicked the knife away, and cast the 'tie-up' spell to bind his feet and hands. Finally, I cast 'forget' spells on both of them, so they wouldn't remember the lightning bolt or the rope trick.

"What did you do to my hand?" he screamed.

"You'll be okay when the paramedics arrive."

"But it's burnt!"

"Stop whining!"

I put my arm around the young woman, and led her outside. She was shaking like a leaf.

"Are you okay?"

She nodded, but didn't look okay.

"You are Amanda, I assume?"

"Yeah."

I put in a call to Maxwell and asked him to send a paramedic.

"You're going to be okay. The police are on their way."

"It's my fault!" She sobbed.

"Don't be silly. You're safe now."

"You don't understand. This is all my fault."

Chapter 23

This promised to be good. Normally, I'd do anything to avoid watching Wool TV, but this morning was Mrs V's first interview which was going to be broadcast live. And her guest was none other than Grandma. I'd made Mrs V promise she wouldn't give Grandma an easy ride, but that she'd push her to talk about Everlasting Wool, One-Size Needles and the one hour delivery promise.

The opening credits rolled before going live to Mrs V who looked totally awesome. The tiara might have been a little much, but still. She appeared to be in Ever A Wool Moment.

"Welcome to V Day. I'm your host, Annabel Versailles. Each week I'll be bringing you all of the hot news and gossip in the racy world of yarn. I'll also be conducting in-depth interviews with the industry's movers and shakers. Which brings me to my first guest. She has taken the world of yarn by storm since she appeared on the scene only a few short weeks ago. She is Mirabel Millbright."

"Who? Mirabel?" I almost spat my cereal over the TV screen. "Are you kidding me? Mirabel Millbright?" It hadn't even occurred to me until now that I didn't know Grandma's name. Never in a million years would I have had her down as a Mirabel. Maybe I should start calling her that? Or maybe I'd rather keep breathing.

What was Grandma wearing? It looked remarkably like the wedding dress she'd tried to wear to my mother's recent wedding, but it had been dyed black.

"Mirabel. Thank you for talking to me today."

Grandma nodded, but said nothing. Was it my

imagination or did she look nervous? I didn't think she did nervous.

"Go get her, Mrs V!" I yelled at the screen.

"Since you opened Ever A Wool Moment recently, you've set the community talking with a number of innovative products. Maybe we should talk about Everlasting Wool? Some people say —"

"I'm glad you mentioned that, Annabel," Grandma interrupted. "Everlasting Wool has indeed proven to be one of our most popular products." She turned to face the camera. "Viewers can sign up for their subscription now at EverAWoolMoment.com. We're running a special offer for viewers of this program — just enter special code 'MRSV', and you'll get a fifty per cent discount on your first month's subscription."

"Some people are concerned about this new approach," Mrs V pushed. "They don't understand how wool can be sold by subscription."

"Some people will always be afraid of change, Annabel, but for those who aren't, you can subscribe to Everlasting Wool at EverAWoolMoment.com. And don't forget to enter the code: 'MRSV'."

"You still haven't addressed the question of how wool can be sold this way."

"It's very simple, Annabel. You pay a monthly subscription and you need never run out of wool again. To sign up just go to EverAWoolMoment.com and enter the code 'MRSV'."

I was yelling at the TV. "Don't let her off the hook! Make her answer the question!"

Mrs V tried, but Grandma ran rings around her. She turned every question into another opportunity to promote her products and her web site. The woman was a genius.

By the time the closing credits rolled, Grandma was all smiles, and Mrs V looked angry and frustrated.

My phone rang.

"Did you see that?" Kathy was buzzing.

"It was terrible. Poor Mrs V."

"What do you mean? It was brilliant. Your grandma is a freaking genius. I've just checked the order log—the sales are through the roof."

"I don't know why you're so pleased."

"She promised me a bonus at the end of the year if we hit our targets."

"'Our' targets? I thought you were the hired help?"

"Gee thanks, Jill. Way to make me feel good about my new career."

"Sorry. I didn't mean that. It's just—"

"Got to go. One of the kids is crying."

She was lying of course, but I couldn't blame her. Just because Grandma was getting under my skin didn't mean I should take it out on Kathy. I'd call her back later when she'd cooled down. What? Yes, of course I'd apologise. I wasn't above apologising. When I'm in the wrong, I'll always apologise. It just so happens I rarely am. Wrong—that is.

***

I'd arranged to meet Daze at Cuppy C, but I stopped off at Aunt Lucy's first. I found her staring out at the garden.

"Aunt Lucy? Are you okay?"

"Sorry, Jill. I didn't hear you come in. I'm fine. The lawn isn't though. Look!"

"The goat?"

"Yes. By the time the spell had worn off, the damage had already been done."

"How was the reporter?"

"He didn't hang around. He said he didn't feel well. Probably all the grass he ate."

"Have you seen Grandma?"

Aunt Lucy rolled her eyes. "I've only just got rid of her. She came here straight from her interview on Wool TV. I suppose you saw it?"

I nodded.

"I feel sorry for your Mrs V. Grandma made mincemeat of her. She was full of it when she was here."

"You know she's using magic in that shop of hers, don't you?"

Aunt Lucy glanced around. "You have to be careful what you say."

"How else could she be doing it? Everlasting Wool? One-Size Needles?"

"Maybe so, but she's family. *Your* family. Don't ever forget that."

Aunt Lucy was right. I had a family now — a family I hadn't even known existed. Why was I trying to sabotage my relationship with them just because Grandma got up my nose? I had to step back. Take a deep breath. I wouldn't let Grandma rile me from now on.

"I thought I saw you arrive." Grandma waltzed into the kitchen. "Come to congratulate me on my TV performance?"

Deep breath. Keep cool. "Morning, Grandma. Yes, I saw

your interview."

"Annabel thought she could ambush me." She scoffed. "What a joke!"

"It was her first show."

"Last one too, probably."

Deep breath. Stay calm.

"What's wrong with your lawn, Lucy?" She stared out of the window.

"The goat. Remember?"

"Oh yes." She cackled. "I'd forgotten about him. Anyway, I've just heard they've given the place in the Hall of Fame to one of the other nominees. Good thing too. I don't want some 'old biddy' award. Oh well, you two look as much fun as a disco at a funeral parlour. I'll go and find some of my fans—sign a few autographs, that kind of thing. And Lucy, get that lawn sorted out. It looks a mess."

With that she was gone.

Aunt Lucy turned to me. "Forget everything I said. Family is way overrated."

Aunt Lucy and I sat down with cups of tea and custard creams. We spent the first ten minutes discussing all the things we'd like to do to Grandma, but then moved on to more pleasant matters.

"There is something I wanted to run by you," she said. "I'm not sure what to do about it."

I was intrigued.

"I've had an approach," she said, in almost a whisper. "From an agent."

"What kind of agent?"

"Agent might not be the right word. I guess he's more

of a middleman. He asked if I'd be interested in baking birthday cakes to order."

"Would you?"

"The extra money would come in handy, and I do enjoy baking."

"So what's stopping you?"

"I'm worried I'll upset the twins. When they first opened Cuppy C they asked if I'd bake cakes for them, but they'd expect me to do it for free. I said no. It's their business and I thought they should have to stand on their own feet. If I say yes to this and they find out, they'll be on my case again."

"Do they have to know?"

"Maybe not. They never pay much interest to what I'm doing anyway, so if I don't tell them—"

"I say go for it. I won't say anything to them."

"You're right. I think I will. Thanks, Jill." She gave me a peck on the cheek. "It's nice to have someone to run this kind of thing past. I would have asked your mother, but she's too loved up with Alberto at the moment."

***

At Cuppy C, Amber and Pearl were doing their best to eavesdrop until Daze gave them one of her looks. That did the trick. Daze had brought along her young sidekick, Blaze. Daze was eating a blueberry muffin. It was the last one, and she'd beaten me to it by seconds. Not that I minded. It did look super delicious though.

"I hope you don't mind that I brought Blaze with me today?"

"Not at all. Good to get the old music hall act back

together again." What? I couldn't help myself.

She gave me 'the look'.

"Sorry. Slip of the tongue. Look, before we get on to TDO business, can I run something else by you?"

"Sure, but first I need a top-up. Blaze, do you mind?"

Blaze sighed, but picked up Daze's cup and joined the queue at the counter.

"Do you remember I told you about a witch who might be abusing her magical powers in the human world?"

Daze nodded.

"Can we keep this just between you and me?"

"Of course."

"I don't know — maybe I should — "

"You're talking about your grandmother, aren't you?"

"How did you know?"

"It wasn't difficult to work out."

"Look. I know this makes me look bad, but I really want to get her out of Washbridge. She's driving me insane. I can put up with her here, but not there as well."

"You'll have your work cut out. To bring her down is going to require cast iron proof. I can't just arrest a level six witch on your say-so. I'd lose my RR licence. Do you have any proof?"

"She's selling wool that supposedly goes on forever."

"That's not proof — it's a subscription."

"You know as well as I do that it has to be magic. How else does a ball of wool keep on going no matter how much you use?"

"I still need proof. If you're serious about this then you're going to have to come up with much more."

I sighed. "Okay. I thought I'd run it by you anyway."

"No problem."

"There you go," Blaze put the coffee on the table in front of Daze.

"Where's my Victoria sponge?" Daze said.

"You never asked for one."

"You know I always have a Victoria sponge with my first refill."

Blaze sighed a huge sigh, and then rejoined the queue.

"Okay," Daze said. "Let's talk TDO. Has he made any more attempts on your life?"

"Yeah. He tied up my cat, Winky, and replaced him with a doppelganger who tried to rip my throat out."

"Nice."

"Winky wasn't impressed."

"Have you made any headway with your investigation?" Daze took a sip of her refill.

"No, but I think we've been approaching this from the wrong angle."

"How do you mean?"

"To find TDO, we have to get at him through his supporters."

"You mean Followers?"

"No. From what I've seen of them, they're little more than androids. I'm talking about the sups that openly support TDO."

"I don't know of anyone who does that."

"I do. Do you remember I took part in the Levels Competition?"

"I heard you did okay."

"I nearly didn't make it there at all. A witch named Alicia Dawes poisoned me. If it hadn't been for Grandma I would probably have died."

Daze raised her eyebrows. "And now you want to have

her arrested?"

"I know, I know. I'm a terrible person. Don't try to make me feel any worse about Grandma than I already do. Anyway, Alicia said something about there being forces much greater than hers that didn't want me in Candlefield."

"That could mean anything."

"I know, but I have a feeling about this. Call it a P.I.'s intuition if you like. Anyway, it's not like I have any other leads. I'm going to do some digging around to see what I can find out about my friend Alicia."

"Do you know anything about her?"

"Not really. Grandma said she comes from a long line of evil witches. And if Grandma thinks they're evil, I guess they really must be. The first thing I need to do is to find out where she lives."

"I may be able to help with that."

"Really? That would be great."

"I can't promise anything, but if she's as bad news as you say she is then it's likely she may have a police record."

"And you can get hold of that?"

"Officially? No. Unofficially? We'll see."

Chapter 24

The phone call had come out of the blue. Dexter Banks' P.A. had asked if I'd visit her boss at his home on Sunday morning. I'd agreed, mainly because I was keen to find out how Amanda was doing.

The house, more a mansion really, was located halfway between Washbridge and Carlton. The area was known locally as millionaires' row, where you wouldn't find any properties for under two million. The house was surrounded by a high wall with CCTV cameras along its length. A security guard with a Special Forces physique and haircut checked my ID before allowing me through the electronic gates. Good job my fuel tank was full because the driveway was almost as long as the drive from my flat. A Rolls Royce, a Bentley and a Ferrari were parked in front of the house. I felt embarrassed to park alongside them.

I'd no sooner stepped out of the car than I heard a familiar voice. "Jill, welcome!"

"Bob? I didn't realise you'd be here."

"Neither did I. Don't get invited up here very often. Not that I'm bothered." He grinned.

"How's Amanda?"

Before he could answer another man appeared in the doorway.

"You must be Jill. I'm Dexter Banks." He shook my hand. "Let's go inside, Patty is keen to meet you."

I followed him across the huge entrance hall to an equally large reception room at the rear of the house. Patty Dale was classically pretty with an elegance money can't buy. She took my hand in both of hers.

"Thank you so much for bringing our little girl back to us."

"I'm just glad everything turned out all right."

"Thanks to you it did," Bob said. "I'm not sure it would have if we'd left it to the police."

"Would you like a drink?" Patty asked.

"I'll have a coffee, please."

"Nothing stronger?" She pointed to the bar in the far corner of the room.

"No, thanks. It's a little early for me."

For the next hour, Dexter did most of the talking. He was a man who liked the sound of his own voice. Although he and Patty couldn't thank me enough for finding Amanda, I found it curious that neither of them had mentioned her whereabouts. Nor was there any mention of Amanda's part in the 'kidnap'. I figured it would be better for me to talk to Bob about Amanda if I could get him on his own.

"Well, I should be making tracks," I said. I'd heard about as many of Dexter Banks' stories as I could take.

"Thank you again." Patty gave me an uncomfortable hug and a peck on the cheek.

"Before you go," Dexter said. "You must allow me to pay you for the work you put into rescuing Amanda."

"Steve hired me. You can pay his bill if you'd like?" Bob had already offered to pick up the tab, but why shouldn't Dexter pay? He could afford it.

I noticed Dexter's expression change momentarily at the mention of Steve's name.

"Of course. Have the bill sent to me would you? I'll take care of it, plus a bonus to show our gratitude."

"That's very kind."

"And if I can ever do anything for you, anything at all—don't hesitate to ask."

"Thank you."

Dexter and Patty waved us off at the door. Bob Dale climbed into the Bentley, and said quietly, "Take a left out of the gates, and meet me at the Coach Inn—it's three miles down the road."

***

I sipped on my soda and lime; Bob took a long drink of his beer.

"I was ready for that." He took a deep breath. "I find Dexter rather tiring."

"He has a lot to say for himself."

"You're lucky. You caught him on one of his quieter days."

"Where's Amanda? How is she? Dexter never mentioned where she was."

Bob laughed. "He's not very happy because she's back with Steve."

"Really?"

"Those two were made for each other."

My first impressions of Steve had proved to be correct. He was a thoroughly decent guy who was madly in love with Amanda. She was lucky to have him, and even luckier that he'd taken her back after she'd almost landed him in jail.

"I hope he knows what he's doing," I said.

"Amanda acted stupidly. She knows that, and she's likely going to pay the price."

"Have the police charged her?"

"Not yet, but they will." Bob shook his head. "She's lucky Dexter not only has money, but has influence in high places. She may get away with a suspended sentence or probation. I still can't understand how she allowed herself to get caught up in something so stupid."

"The answer to that is simple: Tom. He set up the meeting between himself, Steve and Rachel. They were meant to be discussing Amanda's surprise birthday party. Tom cried off, supposedly because he was busy. In fact, he'd planned all along to take Amanda there so she'd see Steve with Rachel. Tom told Amanda the two of them were seeing each other behind her back."

"Why didn't she just confront Steve?" Bob asked.

"I don't know. She obviously wasn't thinking straight. Plus, Tom was telling her what to think and what to do. She went along with the kidnap plan primarily to get back at Steve. She wanted to hurt him. Tom had persuaded her she should start afresh, and that the cash would allow her to do it. Plus it had the added attraction of getting back at her father who she'd never got on with."

"What tipped you off?"

"Mainly Tom. I sensed something wasn't right about him the first time I met him, and his ex-girlfriends confirmed my suspicions. But also the ransom note. No one saw it being delivered—Dexter just found it. Amanda had left it somewhere where she knew her father would eventually discover it—the only surprising thing was it took him so long."

"What do you think would have happened if you hadn't found her?"

"We'll never know, but Tom is a violent man with a track record of abusing women. I doubt he ever had any intention of sharing the money with Amanda. Steve was already suspected of murder. If Amanda had 'disappeared' then he'd probably have been charged eventually."

"What about the phone in Steve's locker, and the tee-shirt?"

"Tom bought the burner phone and had Amanda send the text. It was easy to plant it in Steve's locker. He got Amanda to cut her finger and let it bleed on the tee-shirt. He'd been planning this for some time—ever since he realised who Amanda was, and that her father was rich. Incidentally, have you heard from Rachel?"

"She and Amanda have made up too. Amanda is a very lucky person. Not everyone would have been as forgiving as Steve and Rachel have been. Her biggest break was that Steve came to you. If it hadn't been for you, Tom could have got away with this, and goodness knows what might have happened to her then."

"I'm pleased everything worked out," I said.

"What Dexter said back there—that applies double for me. If ever you need anything, and I mean anything at all, you call on me."

"There is one thing actually."

"Name it."

"I'd love a packet of salt and vinegar crisps. I'm starving."

***

"You'll never guess what!" Kathy yelled down the phone.

"You've decided to give me back my beanies?"

"No. I have exciting news."

"That's nice."

"Aren't you going to ask me what it is?"

"What's your exciting news, Kathy?"

"See, now you've gone and spoiled it."

"I'm sorry. What's your news?"

"I don't know if I should tell you now."

I sighed.

"Go on then." She was bursting to tell me. "I've been promoted again!"

"Already? What to? Chief Knit?"

"Thanks. I might have known you'd make fun."

"I'm sorry. I didn't mean it. So what's the new title?"

"I'm now the shop manager."

"I thought you were only part-time?"

"I've agreed to increase my hours. I'm going to work every day while the kids are at school. It's more money too. She says it will free her up to concentrate on new innovations like the 'Everlasting Wool'."

"Yeah, I just bet it will," I said under my breath.

"What?"

"I said, that sounds great. I'm really pleased for you."

"I can't wait to tell Pete tonight. Anyway, better go I have yarn to manage."

The call made me question whether I was doing the right thing in trying to find evidence against Grandma. If I did, and it was a big 'if' because Grandma was a smart cookie. But if I did, what would happen to the shop if Daze forced Grandma out of the human world? It would most likely shut, and then Kathy would be out of a job. How could I do that? I couldn't. I'd just have to learn to put up with Grandma for now.

It wouldn't be easy.

***

Mrs V popped her head around the door. "I meant to mention. Detective Maxwell called earlier. He wanted you to go to the police station at two o'clock."

"It's ten to two now."

"Sorry. G called and I forgot all about it."

"Right. I'd better get going." I grabbed my bag. "See if you can cheer up the cat."

"How am I meant to do that?"

"I don't know. Tell him some jokes."

There was only one way I'd make it to the police station on time. I cast the 'faster' spell and set off at full pelt.

"I'm here to see Jack, I mean Detective Maxwell." I was still trying to catch my breath. The clock on the wall showed a minute to two.

"What happened to your hair?" Jack said, as he ushered me into our favourite interview room. "You look like you've been in a wind tunnel."

"It's blowing a gale out there," I lied. I could hardly tell him that I'd just been running at the speed of light.

"Strange. I went out earlier, and I didn't notice it."

"Weather?" I managed a weak laugh. "Who can understand it?"

"I thought we should talk about the Banks kidnapping," he said.

I'd been dreading this. "Look, I know I probably should have kept out of it, but—"

He held up his hand to stop me mid-sentence.

"You did good."

"Sorry?"

"You did good. I'm not sure Amanda Banks would still be alive if you hadn't got involved."

"Oh?"

"But—"

I knew there'd be a 'but'.

"This doesn't change anything. The rules remain the same. You do not do anything which might interfere with our investigations from now on. Understood?"

"Aye, aye, Captain."

He smiled. "After what happened at Camberley, this was the best result we could have hoped for."

"Will you charge Amanda?"

"Not up to me, thank goodness. Money talks, so my guess is she'll never see the inside of a prison."

"She's not a bad kid. Just confused."

"Well, now that's all behind us, I suppose you and I should have an evening out sometime?"

"Bowling?" I grinned.

"No."

"Skating, then?"

"Definitely not. Maybe just a quiet drink. Or you could come around to my place, and I could cook."

I'd laughed before I could stop myself. "Sorry. You can cook?"

"I'll have you know, I'm red hot in the kitchen."

That conjured up images in my mind which really had no right to be there. "Is that right?"

"I'll check my diary and give you a call to arrange a date."

"Okay."

Date? Did he mean date as in the day on a calendar or did he mean a *date* date?

Chapter 25

Daze had come through with the address for Alicia. She'd wanted to accompany me, but I'd insisted on going alone. I'd no intention of confronting the evil cow; the plan was to get inside her apartment and to see what evidence, if any, I could find of a connection with TDO.

When I'd first met her—or at least her alter ego Tess—she'd told me she lived close to the park. In fact she lived the opposite side of Candlefield. It was beginning to look as though everything she'd ever told me was a lie. A part of me would have enjoyed a showdown with Alicia—it was probably only a matter of time before that happened. But today wasn't that day. There were far more important issues at stake. The more time I spent in Candlefield, the more I came to realise just how much impact TDO had. He had to be stopped by someone, and seeing as how he'd decided to pick a fight with me, I might just have to be the person to do it. In truth I had no evidence that Alicia was working for, or connected in any way to TDO. I was working purely on gut instinct.

Fortunately, there were several vantage points which overlooked her flat which was on the second floor. I positioned myself on the same floor of the adjacent block. Most of the flats in that building were empty, so I was able to hang around the landing without attracting any attention.

I wasn't sure whether Alicia was even in. I'd arrived at the crack of dawn with the intention of waiting until I saw her go out, but it was almost midday, and I still hadn't caught sight of her. What if she hadn't come home last night? What if she'd changed address? It was always possible that the address which Daze had given me was out of date. How much longer should I give her?

Then the door of her flat opened, and she stepped out. There were very few people in the world that I truly hated, but Alicia was one of them. When I thought back to how she'd befriended me just so she could poison me – it made my blood boil.

I waited until I saw her come out of the building and walk away. Only when she was out of sight did I scurry down the stairs, across the road, and up to her flat. This building appeared to be fully occupied, so I couldn't afford to hang around outside the flat for long or it would draw attention. I could have just forced open the door using the 'power' spell, but I didn't want her to know I'd been there. The small vent close to the floor, underneath the window was my best bet. I cast the 'shrink' spell, crawled through the vent, and then returned myself to full-size.

I'm not exactly sure what I was expecting, but her flat seemed very 'ordinary'. In fact, I had to begrudgingly admit, she had rather good taste when it came to furnishings and decor. I started in the living room – checking every cupboard and drawer. I found nothing. Next I searched the kitchen – again I drew a blank. There was only one bedroom – where once again, I searched every cupboard and drawer as well as the wardrobe. The only papers I found were bills. Back in the living room, I took another look around. It was beginning to look as though I was going to leave empty-handed, but then I noticed the TV. Two things caught my attention. Firstly it was an old fashion set with a deep back, which seemed at odds with the other modern gadgets in the room. Secondly it was nowhere need a power socket. The back panel was held on a by a single screw which I undid easily with a coin. Inside, all of the electronics had been stripped out. All that was left was the tube itself. And a cardboard folder.

It had a single word written on the front 'Gooder'.

***

"What do you think you are doing?" Alicia burst through the door.

I was too far way from the vent to get out the same way as I'd come in, and besides I didn't want to risk shrinking myself now Alicia was back. I wouldn't have put it past her to squash me into the ground. With the folder held tightly under one arm, I cast the 'shatter' spell which disintegrated the window. I jumped onto the sofa, and from there I leapt through the empty window frame. As soon as my feet hit the ground, I cast the 'faster' spell and sped down the stairs and out of the building. I wasn't sure if Alicia had tried to follow or not because I didn't stop to look back. Only when I was back in the centre of Candlefield did I slow down.

The plan had been to get in and out without leaving any evidence of my presence. Yeah well, so much for that. When I was back in my room above Cuppy C, I opened the folder. Inside were stacks of papers and several photographs of me—some taken in Candlefield and some in Washbridge. A few of them had definitely been taken long before I knew I was a witch. The papers all appeared to be written in either a different language or more likely some kind of code. Either way, I couldn't make any sense of them.

I called Daze and brought her up-to-date.

"So Alicia knows you have the file?"

"Oh, yeah. She certainly knows."

"You could be in danger."

"I think I was already in danger. I'm not sure this will make much difference."

"Let me have the file and I'll get some people to look at it—if anyone can decode it, they'll be able to."

***

I arrived at Aunt Lucy's to find her and Lester on their way out.

"Lester is taking me out for tea and cakes," she said.

"Great! Going anywhere nice?"

"Cuppy C, of course. If we went anywhere else, we'd never hear the end of it. Why don't you join us?"

"No, you don't want me with you."

"Of course we do." Lester twizzled his lopsided moustache, which I was slowly growing accustomed to.

They walked hand in hand, and I walked alongside them.

"Have you any plans to see Drake again?" Aunt Lucy asked.

"No, but I do have a date in Washbridge. Well, at least I think it's a date. I'm not absolutely sure."

"With the policeman the twins told me about?"

I nodded. "Jack Maxwell, yes."

"Didn't you have some kind of run-in with him?"

"You could say that, but I'm hoping that might be

behind us now. Oh, by the way, did you know that Kathy has been given two promotions already? Grandma has now made her the manager of Ever A Wool Moment."

"That's nice for her—I suppose. How do you feel about it?"

"I'm pleased for Kathy, but I preferred it when I only had to deal with Grandma when I was in Candlefield."

"My ears are burning." Grandma appeared, wearing a tee-shirt with the word "EVER" on the front. Underneath it was the URL EverAWoolMoment.com.

"Good morning, mother." Aunt Lucy sighed. "We were hoping you'd join us."

"Nice tee-shirt, Grandma." I stifled a grin.

"I'm pleased you like it because I have one for all of you." She pulled out three brand new tee-shirts, still in the cellophane wrapping, and handed one to each of us.

Aunt Lucy muttered something under her breath.

"Put them on, then!" Grandma said, impatiently.

"I am not going out for tea wearing this thing." Aunt Lucy held out the tee-shirt as though it was a bag of dog poo.

Lester began to slip off his jacket.

"And neither are you!" Aunt Lucy pulled it back on.

"What about you?" Grandma fixed me with her gaze.

"I—err—I."

"It will be an improvement on that." She pointed at my yellow top.

"What's wrong with this?"

"You look like a lemon. Come on. Hurry up."

I looked to Aunt Lucy for support, but she wasn't going to fight this battle for me.

"I—don't—"

"You don't what?" barked Grandma.

"I don't mind wearing it." I slipped it over my top. What? It's not like I was afraid to refuse. I could have said 'no' if I'd wanted to. It just so happened I found the tee shirt—err—quite fetching.

The twins were standing outside Cuppy C when we arrived. They took one look at me and descended into giggles.

"Did you EVER see anything like it?" Pearl said through tears of laughter.

"I don't think I EVER did." Amber was doubled up.

I gave them both 'the look', but it didn't stop them.

"It's the best tee-shirt I EVER did see."

"I'm glad you like it," Grandma stepped in front of me. "Because I have one for each of you."

The laughter died there.

"But we're working."

"Put them on now."

The twins slipped on the tee-shirts.

"Well I EVER." I laughed.

"Anyway, what are you two doing standing outside?" Aunt Lucy asked.

They both gestured across the road at Best Cakes.

"What's he done now?"

"Come and see."

They led the way across the road. Aunt Lucy and I followed, leaving poor old Lester with Grandma.

"Look!" Pearl pointed to a huge poster.

"They're offering customised birthday cakes."

I glanced at Aunt Lucy, and knew from the look on her face that the cakes in the picture were hers. She caught my eye and shook her head.

"We should be doing this," Pearl said. "You could make them, Mum."

"Yeah." Amber nodded. "You could do much better than these. Look at them. They're amateurish."

While the twins were grumbling to one another, Aunt Lucy whispered to me, "Don't tell them whatever you do."

Just then, someone shouted a warning, and we all looked around. A driverless van was careering down the road, and it was headed straight for Lester.

"Lester! Look out!" Aunt Lucy yelled, but he'd already seen it.

There wasn't time for him to dodge out of the way — it was almost certainly going to crush him against the wall. I couldn't bear to watch, so I closed my eyes.

"Lester!" Aunt Lucy shouted.

I opened my eyes, and expected the worst, but the van had miraculously come to a halt a few inches short of him.

Aunt Lucy rushed over; the twins and I followed.

"Are you okay?" Aunt Lucy threw her arms around him.

"I'm fine, Lucy. Honestly I'm fine."

"What happened?" I turned to Amber and Pearl. "Did Aunt Lucy stop it?"

"No," Grandma said. "Lester stopped it, didn't you?"

Everyone turned to look at him. We all knew that he'd been seeing a specialist because he'd lost his magic powers. So how had he done it?

"I don't know how I did it." Lester smiled. "I just knew I had to."

"This is *your* doing!" Aunt Lucy turned on Grandma.

"I don't know what you mean." Grandma shrugged.

"You made the van roll down the street. You knew Lester would have to use magic to stop it."

"What are you complaining about? It worked didn't it? I couldn't have a daughter of mine dating a magicless wizard, now could I?"

It took the twins and me to hold Aunt Lucy back.

Chapter 26

"What's that?" Barry asked when I took him for a walk the next morning.

What appeared to be a travelling fun fair had set up overnight in the park—right next to the lake.

"It's nothing to interest you."

"Do they have food?" Barry's nose was twitching.

"No, there's nothing for dogs to eat."

"Are you sure? Something smells nice."

"I'm sure. But I have some treats for you back home?"

"How many?"

"A lot."

"Come on then, let's get back."

He'd already had a good run over the other side of the park—so had I—trying to catch him as usual. I was ready to get back because I had a test with Grandma that afternoon. Yay!

I was used to seeing travelling fun fairs back in Washbridge, but I'd never seen one on this scale. There were rides and side stalls of all kinds.

The twins were ultra bubbly when I got back to Cuppy C.

"What are you two so happy about?"

"Didn't you see the fun fair?"

"I could hardly miss it."

"We love fun fairs," Amber said.

"Yeah. We're going this afternoon."

"I don't think so," I said. "Have you forgotten it's Grandma's test."

They looked at each other and giggled. That was never a good sign.

"What have you two done?"

They giggled some more. Now I knew it was bad.

"We sent a message to Grandma to tell her we had both come down with a twenty-four hour bug and wouldn't be able to go to the test."

I laughed. "And you seriously expect her to believe that?"

"She probably will, actually," Pearl said. "because we sent the message from you."

"You did what?"

"We knew you wouldn't mind." Amber stepped behind her sister.

"I do mind! She'll kill me when she finds out that you aren't ill."

"She won't find out. We'll be at the fun fair while you are at the Range. She'll never know."

Would these two ever learn? After the incident with the donkey ears, I'd thought they might actually get a clue, but apparently that was too much to hope for.

"You aren't angry, are you Jill?" Pearl said, nervously.

"I'm not angry—just speechless. Look, I have to go back to Washbridge. I have a cat to feed before the test. You two do what you like."

***

Winky was sulking.

"What's wrong with you?"

"Don't ask."

"Okay."

"Well if you must know. Bella has upset me."

"Has she been semaphoring other cats again?"

"No. We've retired the flags for now. They play hell with my elbow joints."

"Wise decision. So what has she done?"

"She isn't speaking to me."

"What did you do?"

"Nothing."

"Winky?"

"It's true. How can I help it if someone chooses to 'lick' me on FelineSocial?"

"When you say *someone*, would that *someone* be another lady cat?"

"Yes. But I didn't encourage her. I barely know Trixie."

"Trixie? Seriously?"

"I like her name."

"So, can't you just 'unlick' her?"

"That would be rude, and besides she's pretty hot."

"Sounds to me like Bella may have cause for concern."

"What would you know?"

"Why? Because I'm not a cat?"

"No because you can't get a man to save your life."

Touche.

***

I expected Grandma to lay into me the moment I arrived at the Range.

"It's a pity the twins are poorly," she said. "I hope they get better soon."

Huh?

"Still, at least you made it."

This wasn't right. Something was terribly wrong. Surely Grandma hadn't fallen for the message which had supposedly come from me? I'd expected her to be on the war path, talking about all the things she was going to do to the twins.

We spent the whole session on a single spell—the 'move' spell. She set me task after task with different objects. Some of the tasks required an incredible amount of precision, but by the end, I felt as if I had acquitted myself well. Whether Grandma did was of course another matter entirely.

"You did well today, Jill"

What? Had I just heard correctly?

"Credit where credit is due, you seem to have mastered that particular spell."

"Err—thanks."

She made me nervous when she was being nice—or at least what passed for 'nice' for Grandma.

"You didn't let the twins' absence put a damper on it," she said. "And anyway that's water under the bridge. After all, this one test is just a mere drop in the ocean."

Now she was rambling. It wasn't like Grandma to talk in cliches, but, it was better than having her tear the usual strip off me.

***

When I got back to Cuppy C, I saw the twins walking up the road. Something about them wasn't right. I'd expected them to be all giddy and excited after their jaunt at the fun fair. Instead they were slouched over as though they had all the troubles in the world on their shoulders. As they got closer, I realised that something else was amiss. They were both soaked to the skin.

"What happened to you two?"

"We were in the lake." Amber squeezed the sleeve of her tee-shirt.

"Why did you go in the lake with your clothes on?"

"It's not like we chose too," Pearl snapped.

"Sorry. So what happened? Did you fall in or something?"

"I need to get a shower and get changed." Amber pushed past me.

"Me too." Pearl followed.

An hour later, they had showered, changed and were in much better humour.

"Sorry we snapped at you," Amber said. "It wasn't your fault."

"Yeah, sorry." Pearl took a sip of coffee. "We shouldn't have taken it out on you."

"That's okay, but I still don't understand what happened."

"We were having a great time. We'd been on the big wheel and the dodgems."

"Yeah, and had a toffee apple too."

"Then we decided to go in the bubbles."

"The what?"

"That's what they call them. They're a kind of clear, plastic bubble which goes on the lake. You get inside and kind of walk on the water. They're fun."

"Until they ripped open," Amber said.

"The bubble burst?"

"They both did. They only allowed one person in each bubble. Mine burst and then Amber's burst a second later. We both ended up in the lake."

"Did you complain?"

"Of course we did, but the owner couldn't understand it. He said that they'd been using them for over four years and not a single one had burst before."

"That's unbelievable," I said. "I'm really sorry."

Grandma's words came back to me: '*You didn't let the twins' absence put a damper on it. And anyway that's water under the bridge. After all, this one test is just a mere drop in the ocean.*'

I almost stopped myself laughing, but not quite.

***

By the time I got back to my flat in Washbridge, I was exhausted. Still, it had been a good day. I had a date with Jack Maxwell to look forward to, and Lester had his magical powers back—even if Grandma's methods had left a lot to be desired. All was well with the world.

"Hi, Jill."

Spoke too soon. "Hi, Betty."

"Have you seen him?" she said.

"Who?"

"The new neighbour. He moved in earlier today."

"No, not yet." I wasn't in any hurry to either.

"He's hot." Betty's face glowed. She was obviously smitten. A tax inspector and a bookkeeper—the perfect match.

"I've no doubt I'll bump into him sooner or later." Unfortunately.

"He even has a hot name." Betty practically swooned. "Luther Stone."

ALSO BY ADELE ABBOTT

The Witch P.I. Mysteries:

The Susan Hall Mysteries:

Whoops! Our New Flatmate Is A Human.
Whoops! All The Money Went Missing.
Whoops! There's A Canary In My Coffee
See web site for availability.

AUTHOR'S WEB SITE

http:www.AdeleAbbott.com

FACEBOOK

http://www.facebook.com/AdeleAbbottAuthor

MAILING LIST

(new release notifications only)
http:/AdeleAbbott.com/adele/new-releases/